"I have a job to do."

"Well, do it and leave," she told him.

Jake shrugged. "I can't. You refuse to cooperate."

"Fine, be stubborn."

"I'm not. It's just—"

"Just what?"

Kenzie was spitting mad now, he could tell...and she looked more adorable than ever.

"Jake Scott, you drive me crazy."

He couldn't help the smile that came from somewhere deep within him. She sounded exactly like that feisty girl with the heart of gold he'd fallen for all those years ago. "Kenzie Grant, I sometimes believe that's my whole purpose in life."

She let out a throaty little groan and then abruptly disappeared inside the farmhouse. Next, the porch window they shared was slammed shut so hard the lamp beside his bed bounced off the table and landed on the floor, shattering the bulb.

"So not my finest moment," he muttered and looked up at the starry night sky and prayed.

Dear Reader,

The Grant family, comprised mostly of women, is at it again in this story of childhood rivals. Jake and Kenzie have been trying to outdo each other ever since they first met on his family ranch in Montana, when she was still carrying around a doll in her back pocket and he was dreaming of rodeos.

Now that they're all grown up, that rivalry hasn't stopped. Matter of fact, it gets stronger when Kenzie learns Jake has been called in to help her turn the family ranch into a more "natural" enterprise.

What?

I love writing about a character who has developed his or her own set of rules to live by, and seems to be doing quite well, until someone arrives and upsets the applecart. It always makes for a fun story with lots of soul-searching for each character. Who has to change the most or compromise the most to gain what they ultimately want...true love?

I hope you fall in love with Kenzie and Jake as much as I did while writing about them. Writing an entire story is such a personal experience, one that always amazes me. A character comes up and taps me on the shoulder and says, "It's time you told my story, and it's a doozy!" How can I refuse? I can't, so I begin, and what ends up on the page is me channeling that character. It's something I love to do, and hope you love to read.

All best,

Mary

www.maryleo.com

Facebook: maryleoauthor

Twitter: @maryleoauthor

A COWBOY
TO KISS

MARY LEO

Recycling programs
for this product may
not exist in your area.

ISBN-13: 978-0-373-75764-0

A Cowboy to Kiss

Printed in U.S.A.

USA TODAY bestselling author **Mary Leo** grew up in south Chicago in the tangle of a big Italian family. She's worked in Hollywood, Las Vegas and Silicon Valley. Currently she lives in San Diego with her husband, author Terry Watkins, and their sweet kitty, Sophie. Visit her website at maryleo.com.

Books by Mary Leo

Harlequin American Romance

Falling for the Cowboy
Aiming for the Cowboy
Christmas with the Rancher
Her Favorite Cowboy
A Christmas Wedding for the Cowboy

Visit the Author Profile page
at Harlequin.com for more titles.

Prologue

"You can't be a cowboy. You're a girl," ten-year-old Jake Scott stated as if everyone on the entire planet already knew this fact. Then he rolled his eyes and climbed up the side of the wooden horse corral, his cowboy boots slapping each rung with a loud thump while his small hands expertly grabbed hold, having done this many times before.

When he arrived at the top, he perched himself on the thick rail, swung his feet over it and stared at the three horses his dad had recently purchased. They were taller than most of the other horses he'd ridden, and their height scared him as he watched them prance around the large space in a tight formation. His dad had promised that the brown-and-white paint would end up being his, once the animal was trained, of course. At the moment, Jake couldn't even imagine getting anywhere near the young stallion without his dad close by. The horses had only recently been separated from their moms and were easily spooked in their new surroundings.

"Haven't you ever heard of a *cowgirl*?" Kenzie

Grant countered as she deliberately followed him up the side of the corral, shoving her dumb doll into her back pocket. She never went anywhere without it. Even took it to the roundup. Who brings a doll to a roundup?

As far as Jake could tell, this girl tried her darnedest to irritate his normally easygoing self. Ever since she'd arrived at the ranch with her family of mostly girls, Kenzie had been a constant thorn in Jake's side. Her brother didn't pay him much mind, and her sisters mostly stayed at the house. But Kenzie seemed to stick to him like glue.

There was no getting rid of her. She followed him around all day like a lost baby goat, mimicking his cowboy ways, trying to learn something that no girl, especially a girl who wasn't even nine years old yet, could do as good as a boy.

"Aw, *cowgirl*'s not even a real word," Jake said. "Not really. At least not from where I come from, and I come from Montana, where cowboying is a man's world."

"Then what are you doing playing cowboy? You're not a man. You're just a kid, like I am."

"I gave up *playing* a long time ago, not like you, who still carries around a stupid doll."

"This doll's not stupid. She's smart. And for your information, this is a cowgirl who runs her own ranch…just like I will when I grow up. Don't you know that kids can be anything they want to be? Don't you have any imagination at all, Jake Scott?"

Kenzie pulled herself up on the top rung, carefully

swung each leg over the side, then sat down right next to Jake. Kenzie was tall for her age, and strong, stronger than Jake liked to admit. Plus, she was smart as a whip and could usually figure out even the toughest tasks Jake tried to stump her with.

Kenzie Grant was just plain annoying.

"Sure I do. Like I can imagine myself riding that palomino with the flaxen mane and tail until I'm an old man." He nodded toward the horses, wondering if this newly declared cowgirl even knew which one was the palomino.

"Horses only have a life expectancy of twenty-five to thirty years. You'll hardly be an old man when it dies."

"Who said?"

"My dad, and he knows a lot about horses. He used to raise them, which is exactly what I'm going to do when I grow up. I'm going to raise horses, and run a ranch, my own ranch, with cattle and a bull. We might even grow some potatoes. Idaho is the potato capital of the world."

She stretched out her arms to make her point. Who cared about a dumb ol' potato anyway?

Nobody, that was who. Especially nobody who lived in Montana.

"There you go again. Making no sense. That's not a ranch. That's a farm. Ranchers don't grow anything but livestock."

"I can grow anything I want, and I can do anything I want. All you want to do is ride some ol' horse. You're just jealous 'cause I'm going to be a rancher...a rancher who does it all. Now who's stupid, Jake Scott? I don't want to talk to you anymore today."

Then she twisted herself to get back down the side of the corral.

"So what happens tomorrow? Are you going to talk to me tomorrow?"

He suddenly didn't want her to go. For all her orneriness, he liked having her around. His two brothers were a lot older, so they didn't pay much attention to him, and his mom and dad were too busy with ranching to ask more than a million "did'ja" questions every day... *Did'ja brush your teeth? Did'ja help clean out the stalls? Did'ja finish all your chores...*

"We're leaving tomorrow. Don't you know anything?"

"Then I guess this means we won't be talking at all."

"What do you care? I'm just a dumb cowgirl."

She climbed all the way down, then jumped off the bottom rung and ran off leaving him alone. He wanted to run after her, and turned to do it when he spotted her brother, Carson, coming up to meet her. Jake liked her brother, Carson. He could ride a horse better than any kid he'd ever seen and Jake had hoped that Carson would teach him a few tricks. That probably wouldn't happen now that he'd told Kenzie all that silly stuff about her being a dumb cowgirl. He knew perfectly well that some girls were even better at ranch work than boys. He just didn't want to admit it to Kenzie. She was only eight years old and he'd bet his new boots she was brave enough to ride that palomino his dad had brought home.

He was simply too shy to admit it…and much too shy to admit he liked hanging with her, even if she did carry around a stupid doll.

Chapter One

Kenzie Grant had only one thought on her mind when she walked out the front door that morning: *frozen semen.*

The way she had it figured, it was her best shot. She'd tried other forms of semen and they simply didn't take or the specimen would be rendered useless before she'd even had a chance to use it.

Semen was funny that way, she thought, just as unpredictable as the stud who provided it.

"Are you confident this will work?" she asked her younger sister, the only doctor Kenzie trusted with their future. Coco wore a straw cowgirl hat over her short-cropped dark hair, a deep blue T-shirt, stretch jeans, and high work boots that laced up the front. Kenzie never could understand why anyone would prefer those to slip-on Western boots, but Coco rarely wore anything that didn't lace up. She was the tallest of the four sisters, exactly six feet tall in her bare feet, and usually carted around a Yorkie named Punky. Today, Punky had to stay home. Apparently he was busy keeping a tiny kitten company that someone had recently left on Coco's doorstep. Among Punky's many virtues, he was an excellent babysitter to just about any creature in need, and that included cats of all sizes.

"At this point, it's your safest bet," she told Kenzie, her gaze on the Teton Mountain range off in the distance. It was a particularly beautiful morning in Idaho's Teton Valley, the crisp blue sky dappled with billowy white clouds and the sun bursting through, sending rays of golden sunlight streaming down to the ground in columns of warmth. The temperature had finally risen and Kenzie had dressed for the part in a brown T, boot-cut jeans, her favorite tan boots and a wide belt held in place with the All-Around Cowboy buckle she'd won four years ago at the local ranch rodeo, the belt and buckle riding low on her hips.

Work gloves and her phone were stuffed in one back pocket, and a packet of spicy beef jerky in the other just in case she had to miss lunch, which had been almost every day last week. She was hoping this week would go easier.

Dora and Dolly, the family's yellow Labs, sniffed the ground as they searched for any new scents that may have dropped from the sky overnight, happy to chase after whatever moved in the expanse of grass that surrounded the ranch house.

Never taking these perfect moments for granted, Kenzie pulled in a deep breath, drinking in the fresh, early morning scent that surrounded her. She only wished she had more time to enjoy these long lazy days like she'd had when she was a kid, when the hours seemed endless. She was hopeful that once the family ranch was lucrative again, an occasional lazy afternoon might be possible, but until then, Kenzie had no time for anything other than work and worry.

All ten of her mares were in various stages of estrus or heat, a situation she'd purposely planned for. Granted, the mares were as ornery as June bugs caught in a net, but once they were impregnated, they'd calm down. At least that was the idea. Now all she had to do was inseminate them, and with her sister's help, next summer her mares would be part of the first annual colt auction on the Grant ranch. She hoped to double that count in twelve months' time, and onward until she brought it up to about thirty or forty workhorses for sale each year.

She didn't like to admit it, but full-time ranching was taking its toll. She knew it would be hard from having grown up on the family spread, but now that her dad had handed over the reins, Kenzie wasn't so sure she wanted to handle them entirely on her own. Her parents now depended on her almost 100 percent, which was fine, but the burden of it sometimes weighed her down more than she ever dreamed that it would.

"Good, 'cause I've ordered the semen from a quarter horse ranch out of Canada. Their workhorses are known throughout the country as being some of the best stock," she told Coco.

Coco gazed over at her, her eyebrows knitted together with concern. "I wish you had consulted me on this order first. I thought we decided on a distributor in Colorado. I've recommended them before to other local ranchers and they've been dependable with their deliveries. They've already done all the customs paperwork for you."

"Sure, but what could be better than going directly to the source, right?"

"I've heard there could be problems with customs, causing major delays."

But Kenzie wasn't listening. She'd stopped walking, pulled her deep brown cowgirl hat down low to shield her eyes from the sun and stared at the white three-quarter-ton pickup. The truck was pulling the exact seventeen-foot horse trailer that Kenzie had lusted over just last month when she was in the market for a new one. The price tag had been a little too rich for her, so she'd had to settle for one that was used and half the price.

The thought flitted through her head that perhaps her dad had decided to splurge and had secretly bought it, but that thought was quickly dashed. She knew her dad would never undermine her financial plan for the ranch. He respected her decisions too much.

Still...

"Do you know what this is all about?" Coco asked, nodding toward the fancy rig heading for them.

"No, but maybe Mom does. Now that their anniversary is less than two weeks away we've been getting all sorts of weird things delivered to the ranch. Mom is getting more and more giddy over the ceremony. I'm so glad we were able to convince them to celebrate forty-five years with a real wedding celebration. Who knew they'd never had one?"

"I don't think Dad's excited about all the fuss, but this means so much to Mom that he's coming around. He'll do anything for Mom, we all know that," Coco said. "Her whole face lights up whenever she talks about any of the details. I've had so much fun helping her plan."

"We all have. Just yesterday an older man arrived with four white doves. Mom wants them released during the ceremony. Did you know, they're actually homing pigeons? Anyway, we did a practice run, and the birds squawked the entire time. It wasn't pretty. Or rather, it didn't sound pretty. You can imagine her reaction."

Coco nodded. "She must have been annoyed."

"She was. The man apologized and assured her it had never happened before and would never happen again, but Mom thought it was a bad omen. It took all day for Dad and me to convince her that their wedding ceremony isn't doomed. You know how she's always felt about elaborate weddings. Nervous that something major will go wrong. Where she got that idea she won't say other than it's just a feeling. Of course, it didn't help that Kayla's first and second weddings were disasters. And Carson's wedding was strange, at best."

Their mom and dad had gotten married at the courthouse in a simple ceremony with no guests. She had insisted it be held that way and had always associated a big wedding with a catastrophe.

"Exactly, and with the Grant track record, who can blame her?"

Their sister Kayla had left not one but two separate grooms standing at the altar, and their brother, Carson, had planned a fancy church wedding with a woman who had already dumped him.

"Callie and Joel's wedding turned out okay," Coco reminded her.

"Except for Great-Uncle Peter streaking through the back of the church in his birthday suit during the vows, everything else went off beautifully."

"Oh, yeah, I forgot about Great-Uncle Peter. Will he be coming?"

"Yes, and Great-Aunt Beverly promised to keep a tight rein on him this time."

"Isn't she the one who tried to do a pole dance during the reception, and I had to treat her when she slid too fast, fell over and bonked her head?"

"Yes," Kenzie answered, remembering Great-Aunt Beverly circling the pole with her undies showing, singing "I'm an Old Cowhand." "Mom might be right."

"So, I wonder what this is? Maybe Mom and Dad want to ride in on special horses? White Arabian horses to go with the white doves, maybe?"

Kenzie snickered and shrugged. "Who knows? She's been springing these changes on us for the last couple of weeks. She's also thinking of handing out white helium balloons to everyone to be set free once Mom and Dad say 'I do.' For someone who doesn't believe in elaborate weddings, she's really all in for this one. I've stopped trying to second-guess what she's thinking up next. I just go along with everything. It's simpler."

As the rig came closer, Kenzie's stomach began to

feel queasy, like the bacon and eggs she'd downed in a hurry that morning weren't sitting well. Or perhaps it was the instant coffee she'd made in the microwave before her mom put on a pot?

It didn't help that the dogs seemed skeptical of the intruder as well, their tails still as they sniffed the air for any strange scents.

"That's a Montana plate on the front of the truck. I can't believe she had to go all the way to Montana to find a horse. Something else must be going on," Kenzie offered.

"I know the Scotts are driving in for the wedding. Maybe Jan and Fred decided to show up early?"

Henry Grant, their dad, and Fred Scott had served in Vietnam together, and had a long-standing friendship. The two men would do anything for each other, and over the years, the Grant family and the Scott family had spent time on each other's ranches. For the most part, those visits had been fun, but there was one member of the Scott family Kenzie never wanted to see again. One cowboy she hoped would stay home on the family ranch where he belonged.

The screen door behind them squeaked open, then banged shut. "Right on time," Kenzie's father, Henry, said.

"Dad knew about their early arrival and didn't tell us?" Coco asked her sister. "I would have changed some of my commitments around. As it is, I can't stay. I'm already late for my next appointment."

"I think there's something more to this than just an extended visit from Jan and Fred. When have they ever stayed longer than a few days? And why would they bring along some horses? No. Something's up, and I'm getting a bad feeling about it."

Kenzie glanced back at her mom who'd stepped out on the porch to join their dad. "I better make up another batch of bacon, and throw on some more flapjacks. Prob'ly drove all night and they'll all be as hungry as a bear."

"Why are the Scotts here so early, Dad?" Kenzie shouted back to her dad.

She couldn't imagine why he hadn't told her, especially since it now appeared as if they'd be staying on the ranch. The guesthouse hadn't even been cleaned out yet. Kenzie had planned to have it done by the end of the week. It was on the top of her priority list, along with several other critical items. She'd been storing some combustible supplies in the guesthouse to keep them away from the livestock. She intended to move them to one of the sheds. Plus Carson had been promising to move all his equipment to his own shed at his rented house for weeks now. The timing of their arrival couldn't be worse.

"Ain't the Scotts, at least not all of them. Just one," her dad finally said in that raspy morning voice of his.

Coco raised an eyebrow and caught the look of concern on Kenzie's face. "What's wrong? You look sick."

Kenzie pressed a hand to her stomach and ignored her sister's question.

Instead, she asked her dad, "Which one? I mean, which Scott?"

The words jumped from her mouth in a rush of

adrenalin. There was only one member of the Scott family who got under her skin, one Scott who annoyed her to distraction and caused her blood to boil. Over the years, their rivalry had grown into a full-blown war. The last time they met up Kenzie was sixteen, and somehow that conniving, underhanded Jake Scott had managed to get her to kiss him. She hadn't kissed a boy before that, and Jake knew it as soon as their lips met.

He'd laughed.

Right there in the middle of the kiss, he'd up and laughed.

It was possibly the most embarrassing moment of her life, and because of it, she'd stopped visiting the Scotts. And Jake, thank you very much, never showed up on the Grant Ranch after that. So it couldn't be Jake Scott inside that pickup. It just couldn't. She'd made it as clear as sunshine that she never, ever wanted to see or talk to him again as long as she lived.

"I'm not exactly sure," he told her with that fatherly tone he took on whenever he didn't want to be questioned further.

"I've got to run," Coco said after she glanced at her watch. "Call me with the details. Sounds like our dad has something up his sleeve... Who knows? Maybe it's a surprise for Mom for their anniversary. Think positive."

Then she dashed off to her red SUV parked near the horse barn, started it up and drove past the Scott rig on her way off the property, sticking an arm out and waving at the driver.

Kenzie watched as the Scott truck and trailer came to a stop a few feet away from her. She waited, telling herself that Jake wouldn't dare show up on the Grant ranch with so much time before her parents' anniversary wedding, not after he hadn't shown up for her sister Kayla's three weddings or Carson or Callie's weddings. He could have at least shown up for one of them. His parents and his brothers, Curt and Lucas, had been there for all of them.

Though Kenzie had never married, she'd heard that Jake was married in a private civil ceremony, but no sooner had that news come through that it was known he'd gotten a divorce. It seemed only fitting. No woman in her right mind could live with the likes of Jake Scott, who was no doubt a scoundrel.

She took a deep breath, and headed for the rig, just as the driver's door swung wide open, and a pair of muddy Western boots hit the gravel. The man who wore those boots also wore an open crumpled long-sleeved black-checked shirt, with the sleeves rolled up; a tight black T-shirt that caressed a chiseled chest and a flat stomach; faded jeans, and a cream-colored Western hat that he slipped on his head. A big grin spread across a scruffy chin, and eyes the color of emeralds peeked out from under the wide brim of his low-slung hat.

Dora and Dolly ran to greet him, now excited about this new visitor. The cowboy bent over and gave them both a warm welcome.

Her darn knees went weak just looking at him, and

for a brief moment, she felt swept up in the vision of pure cowboy walking toward her.

"Is that little Kenzie Grant?" the man asked, his deep voice searing her senses.

All she could do was nod.

"Darn, girl!" he said, "C'mon, bring it in closer."

Then he held open his arms and waited for her to step in next to him.

But she didn't.

They stood there for an awkward moment, neither of them really moving.

Everything was happening so fast, it made her dizzy with confusion. She could barely speak, much less allow him to take her in his arms.

"Don't tell me you don't recognize this ol' cowboy? It's me, Jake Scott, the kid you used to follow around like a motherless calf. Look at you." His gaze quickly swept over her body, not in a lascivious way, but in a genuinely friendly way. But she still didn't like it. "All grown up into one fine woman. Still playing cowboy with your fancy hat and your rodeo buckle. And will you get a load of those boots." He whistled while gazing down at her feet. "Must be handmade with all that fancy work going on. Good gracious, you look like that doll you used to carry around in your back pocket."

She resented his disparaging attitude.

"And you look like you slept in your truck."

He tugged at his wrinkled shirt, smiling. "As a matter of fact, I did. But hey, I hear you're runnin' this ranch just like you told me you would. Always did admire that about you."

Kenzie let out the breath she'd been holding as the fuzzy lens slipped from her brain and she could think clearly again. "Admire what?"

"Your spunk. You got it goin' on in spades."

"Thanks, but coming from you, I can't tell if that's a compliment or a barb."

His deep laugh rumbled through her, as his eyes sparkled with the same amount of tease he had when they were kids. "Then nothing's changed between us."

"Should it have?"

"Absolutely straight it should. Come on over here and give this ol' cowboy a big kiss." He stepped in closer, and whispered, "I'm hoping you're a little better at it than you were when you were sixteen."

Kenzie could feel the blood rushing through her veins, could feel the anger exploding in her gut. She wanted to push him away, lash out, tell him what she thought of him, maybe even say something to wipe that grin right off his downright adorable face. Instead, she narrowed her eyes, and said, "I wouldn't kiss you, Jake Scott, if my very next breath depended on it."

"Glad we got that settled right up front, 'cause I was worried you've been pining over me all these years, seeing as how you're still single and all."

Kenzie heard her dad step off the porch. She glanced back at him as he headed toward them. Unlike Kenzie, he looked genuinely happy to see Jake.

"Why don't you keep on going where you're going? We already have a pugnacious bull on this ranch.

There's no room for another one," Kenzie told Jake, a hand resting on one of her hips.

"Can't. First you and me have a little business we need to take care of."

She had no idea what he was talking about, and from the look on his face, he seemed adamant about staying. She folded her arms across her chest.

"You must be mistaken. I don't have any business with you, now or ever."

"Sure you do, and from what I hear, it might take some considerable time to accomplish."

She moved in closer to this misinformed cowboy, so much so that she could smell his musky skin, and feel his breath on her face. Jake Scott had always been taller than she was by at least six or seven inches, but now as she stood not two inches from him, she realized that gap had shrunk to a more perfect fit. Being this close to someone she'd sometimes fantasized about caused a momentary hesitation in her resolve.

Despite her burning rage, she couldn't help the desire that raced through her. She'd always had a thing for Jake, ever since that first summer when they met on his family ranch. That "thing" was more that she'd wanted to be like him: confident, surefooted, smart and perfectly adorable. He even had a small dimple in the center of his chin, from what she could see under all that sexy scruff.

She didn't know why she'd been so attracted to him, or why in some secret way that "thing" still burned bright. Maybe it had something to do with those emerald green eyes of his or that perfect nose, and those tempting lips. Whatever it was, she had no intention of ever giving in to her emotions again… like she had when she was sixteen and she kissed him.

Mistake.

Big mistake.

He smirked and murmured, "Can't keep away from this cowboy, can you? Maybe we should try that kiss again. Might be better now that you're all grown up."

Then he leaned in and she instantly turned away, pressing her lips right up against his ear. "Listen up, you egoist in a cowboy hat. Not only can I kiss you and make your toes curl, but I make love like an alley cat, then purr like a kitten when it's over. I've got a body that's sinfully fabulous, and a mouth that will set your world on fire. Too bad you will never, ever get to even touch my soft, silky, naked skin, much less taste it, you sad excuse for a real cowboy."

Then Kenzie turned on the heels of her very expensive handmade cowgirl boots and strutted away, with an emphasis on some tantalizing hip action. The dogs followed her excitedly.

Eat your heart out, Jake Scott.

JAKE HAD WANTED to make a good impression, especially on Kenzie, and from the look on her face, and from what she'd said, it wasn't exactly what he'd been hoping to make.

From the moment he first saw her as he drove up the ranch road to the main house, he knew he was going to be in big trouble. Not only had she grown into a stunning beauty, but from how her dad had carried on about her, he knew she was an accomplished rancher—albeit a commercial rancher. Which took a lot of hard work, research and knowledge. Not that organic ranching was any easier. It wasn't. But with his hands-on upbringing, and having always lived on an organic ranch, he hadn't had to sit through countless ranching classes in college to learn about what came naturally to him. It was just part of who he'd always been, who he always wanted to be, a rancher.

And now he'd been asked to share that innate knowledge with a woman who'd just told him she made love like an "alley cat."

Why did she have to go and say that?

He couldn't help himself, he felt about as fired up as grease in a hot pan.

He knew he'd have to pull up that little jerk kid she'd known or there'd be no chance of her ever taking his suggestions for the Grant ranch seriously . . . and he prided himself on keeping a level playing field when he had to work closely with someone. It was a rule he'd learned from his dad, and he never let anything get in the way of that, even if he had to go out of his way to be cordial until the job or the partnership was over.

Working with Kenzie Grant couldn't be any different.

What a woman, he thought as he watched her walk away. Too bad he'd been called in to give her suggestions for more natural ranching operations or things might be a lot different. Ever since his divorce over ten months ago, he'd been charging in at full throttle, wanting to assure himself that it wasn't his fault his wife left him before their first anniversary. Now he wasn't so sure. With no one to really confide in, he'd been obsessing over the breakup ever since she'd moved out. He'd never been close enough to his brothers to talk to them about relationships, at least not his own relationships. Being the youngest, advice had never been something he would seek out from his brothers, at least not verbally. He'd learned a lot from them by just observing, but talking over matters of the heart had never been in the cards. He'd always been looked at as the baby of the family. His brothers, Curt and Lucas, were quite a bit older than him, and that gap may as well have been a deep gorge.

Ranching was something else entirely. Both brothers had more or less given that responsibility over to him. He had taken it on because he loved it so much, and it had always come naturally to him, unlike his brothers, who could think of a hundred things they'd rather be doing, especially Curt, who couldn't seem to settle into anything, much less ranching.

Now that his divorce was final, all he wanted to do for the foreseeable future was slow down to the speed of life. Take a break from his everyday routine. Get a new perspective. Take a couple weeks to reflect and come to terms with his current situation.

Single.

I make love like an alley cat.

Oh, yeah, that would slow him down all right... real slow.

"Somehow, I thought my Kenzie would be happy

to see you," Henry Grant said, as he shook Jake's hand then gave him a quick hug.

"We never were kissing cousins," Jake replied.

"More like kissing rivals," Henry said. "Hope that doesn't cause you any problems."

"Nothing I can't handle," he told Henry as he watched Kenzie disappear into one of the longest horse barns he'd seen in a while.

Chapter Two

"What do you mean he'll be staying for a while? Staying where? And for how long?" Kenzie and her father stood in the center of the long horse barn. She had just walked most of the mares out to the corrals and was getting ready to release the last two.

"Here," her dad said, looking a bit sheepish.

"Here, as in on this ranch?"

"Where else? You know the Scotts are always welcome."

"Well, I hope that horse trailer is equipped with a sleeper compartment, because there's no room inside the house, what with my siblings still claiming their bedrooms as their own. You can't just drop somebody in one of their rooms without them knowing about it."

Not exactly the truth. Her sisters Coco and Callie had long since moved their important things out of their shared room to their own homes, and only used that room on the rare occasion when all the sisters wanted to be together. Kayla would typically just share Kenzie's bed. And she couldn't even remember the last time Carson spent the night.

She was betting her dad hadn't really noticed.

"What about the guesthouse?" he asked after a short pause.

She'd known her dad would think of that dang guesthouse. He'd built it special for relatives and the Scotts to use whenever they came to visit.

She shook her head. "It's still loaded down with boxes of Carson's rodeo memorabilia."

That was the truth. She'd been after him for the last two months to get it cleaned out in anticipation of their parents' anniversary party, but he'd always been too busy, or so he said. Her brother had mixed feelings about his Cowboy Days, especially after a near-fatal accident on a dismount following a solid bronc ride. Got his foot caught-up in a stirrup. Had to be saved by a rodeo clown who nearly died when the bronc Carson had been riding kicked him straight in the chest.

Carson didn't like to be reminded of that time, despite his having moved on. Kenzie feared he'd never get around to moving those boxes to his own shed in town where he lived with his wife, Zoe. But at the moment, Carson's procrastination was proving to be a good thing.

"Jake can sleep out on the bed on the enclosed porch. Your mom can fix it up nice for him."

No way did she want Jake Scott bedding down anywhere on their property, and she especially didn't want him only steps away from her own bedroom.

She didn't understand any of this, and had a hard time believing Jake would want to hang around the

Grant ranch for "a while." And what the heck defined "a while," anyway?

"Why would he want to spend more than one night? Isn't he just passing through? Doesn't he have his own ranch to tend to? And why would he bring his horses with him? What's going on, Dad?"

"I can't answer all them questions at once. Maybe you should come on inside where we can talk, where we can sit a spell. Your mom can brew up a fresh pot of coffee or maybe a nice hot cup of tea might be better."

This mystery was now getting out of hand. She wondered if her dad and Jake's dad hadn't struck some kind of agreement, some kind of bargain that might turn everything she was doing for the ranch into something she wasn't prepared to handle, like maybe a sale. Maybe her dad was thinking of selling the ranch to the Scott family? Was that it?

"I don't want to sit 'a spell.' Tell me here. Now. What's this all about? You wouldn't make some sort of financial deal with the Scotts and not tell me, would you?"

"Never. You're runnin' the show now, not me. But there's one thing I'd like to, well, make a couple changes to. That's why we should go inside where we'll be more comfortable. Your mom can put the tea kettle on."

"I don't want any tea. I have a lot of work to do today, beginning with cleaning out these stalls."

She tossed the clean straw against the walls with her pitchfork, and moved everything soiled to the center. Then she used a shovel to pick up what had been piled in the center and dumped it into the small manure spreader she'd moved to the front of the stall.

"I called him in to help you," her dad said, picking up a broom and sweeping up anything that had fallen from her shovel.

She quickly swept out the center of the stall once all the soiled straw was gone, sprayed an absorbent deodorizer on any wet spots on the rubber mats, and went on to the next stall, allowing the previous one to dry while her mares were outside.

"You asked Jake to leave his own family ranch to come and help me? I thought you liked how I'm handling things. For the first time in years we're making a profit again. I don't understand. Isn't that what you wanted?"

Kenzie had worked out a plan for the ranch down to the smallest detail, which included how to care for each stall. She'd learned from experience that right before she'd bring her mares in for the night, she'd move the good straw back into the center, and add whatever straw was needed to make a soft bed. It took a little longer to care for each stall this way, but she was proud of the fact that her animals had never had any hoof problems since she'd been in charge.

"Of course it is. I just thought—"

She stopped cleaning and stared at her dad, a tall, slim man with kind eyes and graying hair: the textbook cowboy who couldn't be away from his ranch for more than a few days at a time. When Kenzie thought back, she couldn't remember her parents ever taking a vacation. The only place they would visit was the Scott Ranch a few miles outside of Starlight Bend, Montana, and even that had stopped in the last few years.

"I don't need his help, Dad. I already hired two ranch hands to come in three days a week. They've taken over some of the major work, repairing our vehicles, feeding and checking on the livestock, especially our new calves, and mending the holes in our fences. So far they've done a great job. The high school kids who normally help out took the day off to practice for the Cowboy Days next week. Besides, doesn't Jake have his own work to do back in Montana? How can he possibly take off any time to come and help me…do what? Mend a fence? Clean out stalls? Unload hay?"

"It's not that kind of help he's offering."

She punched the pitchfork into the ground and held it taut in her right hand. She didn't know what the heck her dad was getting at, but the knot in her stomach seemed to be getting worse.

"Then what can he possibly be offering?"

Her mind spun to the bedroom, but she instantly tamped that thought down.

"I asked him to give you a few pointers."

"Dad…please spit it out. What kind of pointers?"

He sucked in a deep breath, then let it out. She could tell he was nervous about what he was about to say, but she didn't understand why. She and her dad had an open, honest relationship. At least that was what she thought they had. At the moment she wasn't so sure.

"Pointers on a more organic, more natural method of ranching."

Goose bumps appeared up and down her arms as her stomach tightened. "What? Dad? You can't be serious. I've…"

He held up his hands. "Now, wait. Before you go gettin' all riled up, just listen to me for a minute."

"I've brought this ranch back from the brink. We're doing really well. You know how hard I work."

"And I appreciate that. I'm mighty proud of you and all that you've done. I'm just sayin' that maybe we can go back to a few of the more natural ranchin' ways, some of the old Western ways of doin' things. I'm not too happy about spreading all them chemicals on our crops or using artificial means to impregnate some of our livestock. I'd like the simpler way, the cowboy way."

She took this as a real insult to all that she'd learned, and all that she'd done so far to keep the ranch out of bankruptcy. Didn't her dad understand that?

"Those natural ways weren't working for us, Dad. You know that. We were in debt, a lot of debt, and we came close to losing this ranch. I'm trying to get us some purebred quarter horses. And I don't want any inbreeding with our studs. I want to do this right this time."

"I'm convinced now that a lot of this ranch's decline was because your mom and me just got too old and couldn't take care of everything like we once did. And some of it might have been because we weren't doing things right. Maybe Jake can show us a better process, tell us what we can change or add to what you're already doing. I'd like to start with the stud quarter horses he's brought."

"And who told him to bring those darn studs?"

"Nobody. I offered, and your dad agreed." Jake's booming voice echoed behind her.

"Dad—" She stared at her father for a moment, shaking her head. He simply didn't understand what she was trying to do, and now he was telling her she should listen to a man who probably knew more about wooing a woman than he knew about actual organic ranching…which had to be more expensive and time-consuming than her dad could ever imagine.

"And I'm not charging stud fees," Jake added. She could hear the condescending innuendo in his voice. As if this was all some sort of joke…at least that was how it sounded to her.

"That's not the point," Kenzie argued, unable to fully understand why her dad had gone behind her back. She felt completely betrayed. What could he possibly have been thinking by not discussing trucking in Jake Scott and his stud horses?

"The point is," Jake countered, "my boys are ready, willing and better still, they're already here. And from the looks of some of your twitchy mares out there, they're interested in these guys…so to speak."

A shiver went up Kenzie's spine as she watched Jake walking up to her, guiding what had to be the most beautiful palomino she'd ever seen. Her mind raced back to the palomino she'd seen on Jake's ranch when they were kids. Could this be the same horse?

"Is this Running Star?" Kenzie asked, momentarily forgetting about the span of time that had gone by since she'd last seen the horse.

Just the sight of such a beautiful cream-colored creature caused her to also forget about the ongoing argument. All she wanted to do was run a hand over what had to be the smoothest coat she'd seen in a long time. The horse was positively magnificent, and if she hadn't already paid for frozen sperm, she'd match up this stallion with her mare Sweet Girl in a heartbeat.

The horse nodded its majestic head a few times, as if it knew what she'd been thinking.

"No. Running Star is too old to stud out, but he sired this fella. Morning Star is just about three years old and in top form."

Jake stroked the animal's shoulder, and the horse nuzzled him and nickered.

Kenzie leaned the pitchfork against a stall gate and ambled over to Morning Star, running her hand over his smooth muscular body when she stepped close enough. Then she pulled a small apple out of a sack that hung on a hook between two stalls and held it out to him. Morning Star gently plucked it from her hand, a true gentleman of a horse.

"He's a sweetheart," she told Jake. "What a beautiful animal."

"He'd be a sweetheart to your mares as well," he answered. "He was pasture bred, and is trained to do the same. I can introduce him and Bingo to your mares, and, well, within no time, even your lead mare will foal."

She stepped away from the stallion. "As tempting as that sounds, that's not the haphazard strategy I intend to use. In order to keep this ranch moving in the right direction, I've made other plans for my mares. And besides, there's always a risk with pasture breeding that one of my mares might get injured, or worse. I can't afford to take that chance. This ranch can't afford to take that chance.

"As pretty as he is, I'm going to have to pass on your generous offer. Besides, I've already invested several thousand dollars in pedigreed frozen sperm that will be arriving any day now. It's the safest way to go."

"According to whom?"

"According to other breeders."

"Commercial breeders. I'm talking about natural breeders, and they all agree with pasture breeding. Plus, it's much more fun for the animals than a metal vagina and a long syringe."

"You make it sound so crude and heartless."

He raised an eyebrow. "Well, it sure ain't the way nature had intended it."

Henry cleared his throat. "I'll be gettin' on back to the house now."

Kenzie turned to him. "Is there anything else you want to say before you go, Dad? Maybe ask Jake here to pack up and leave in the morning? That we won't be needing him or his fancy studs?"

He shook his head. "Nope. Wouldn't be hospitable of me to ask him to leave so soon. He'll have to decide that on his own. Both of you will. I'm confident you two can work out the comings and goings of this here idea of mine. Till then, I'm hoping for the best."

Then her dad hightailed it out of there, leaving Kenzie to deal with Jake all on her own.

"So," Jake said as a self-satisfied smirk stretched across his fine lips, "when do we start mating?"

BY THE TIME Jake settled in his bed on the back porch that night, just on the other side of Kenzie's open window, he was more tired than a mule after a day of pulling a plow. It had been not only a long day of driving, but a long day of trying his best to not cause a dustup between himself and the woman he was tasked with helping. Although as it stood at the moment, her accepting his help seemed about as likely as pigs flying.

The porch bedroom had all the accoutrements necessary for his comfort. The only problem was the area was designed for someone five inches shorter, and about fifty pounds lighter. He felt like the proverbial bull in a china shop. Every time he moved, he either knocked something over or bumped into a delicate piece of furniture. Everything seemed to be woven out of wicker and the chair would certainly split apart if he decided to sit on it and put his feet up on the rickety-looking stool.

The one thing he really liked, however, was sleeping essentially outdoors. There was a roof to shelter him from the rain, and the entire area was screened off in order to keep the flying bugs away. There was a wooden rocking chair in the corner that looked a bit more sturdy to sit in, a single-sized bed ran along the wall and ended under the window, an old wooden dresser stood on the other side of the window, with a hook above it to hang his hat, and a small nightstand was next to the bed for his keys and wallet. The small table also held a digital clock, a glass of water and a small frilly lamp. Everything he needed was in a space no bigger than one of those horse stalls in the barn, and even those were probably bigger.

"Are you going to keep that light on all night?" Kenzie called through the open window.

Trying to sleep on a single bed that was obviously made for a shorter person, and was about as wide as his shoulders, while Kenzie Grant lay about ten feet away from him in a comfortable-looking queen-sized bed— he'd peeked in through the curtainless window—was proving to be more uncomfortable than resting his head on his saddle while lying on the cold hard ground…in a rainstorm…without a tarp.

"I like to read before I go to sleep," he answered. "It clears my thoughts and puts me in a sleepin' mood."

As if that was even possible tonight.

At the moment he was reading a thriller by Steve Berry, only for the life of him, he couldn't remember what it was about.

Kenzie poked her head through the window. "Do you think you can do your reading somewhere else?"

He looked up from his book just as he caught her gaze slipping over his bare chest like a gentle breeze in summer. He couldn't help the grin that captured his alley cat thoughts. "Is that an invitation into your bed? Because if it is, I'm sure we can find other things to do besides reading."

She wore a sleeveless gray T-shirt and from the way her breasts pressed against the fabric, there was no bra restricting their movement. He mentally told himself to calm down, and was thankful for the blankets that covered the bottom half of his body. Her dark hair encircled her face and cascaded off her shoulders. The glow of his lamp highlighted the soft features of her beautiful face.

Oh, yeah, he was ready to sleep all right.

"You're incorrigible, do you know that?"

No truer words…

She started to pull herself back inside until he said, "I'm just lying here minding my own business. You're the one causing the fuss."

She poked her head back out again, and this time she must have knelt on the floor of her room, as she rested her head in the crook of her arm like she was going to stay a spell. "I need it to be dark when I sleep."

She yawned, then excused herself, her eyes filling with tears as she quickly wiped the salty liquid away with her fingers. Kenzie Grant looked like a dream framed in that window…his dream.

"It doesn't seem like you're doing much sleeping

hanging out of your window, ordering me around in my own space."

He couldn't help himself. He enjoyed teasing her. She was so easily riled up.

"A space I was against my dad giving you, but you're our guest, at least for tonight."

She yawned again, covering her mouth with her hand. "Excuse me," she mumbled again, looking all sleepy and content. He wondered what it would feel like to have a sleepy Kenzie Grant resting her head on his chest rather than her own arm.

He suspected it would feel pretty darn good.

"And as your guest," he began, trying to get the imaginary sensation out of his head, "shouldn't you treat me with a little respect?"

"I didn't invite you here."

He tried to get a little more comfortable in his bed, but the more he stirred the more uncomfortable he became, the headboard knocking against the wall with each of his movements.

"No, but your father did, so you're stuck with me."

He put his book down next to him, careful to keep it open to his page, sat up and added another pillow under his back. Then he snuggled in tight to the pillow.

"Only for tonight. You're free to go in the morning."

"Actually, I'm free to go right now."

She sat up and pulled her arm inside. Apparently, she hadn't liked what he'd said.

"Then why don't you?"

He squirmed down farther in his tiny bed. "And

leave all this country hospitality? I'm just now settling in."

His feet popped out of the covers that had been tucked into the bottom of the bed. He felt exactly like an overturned beetle.

She sniggered at his struggle to settle, and he realized it was the first time he'd seen her laugh since he'd arrived, and he liked it…a lot. Her eyes sparkled when she laughed and her face lit up, despite any harsh words that might pour out of her mouth.

"I'm sure you would be much more comfortable in your own bed…in your own house…in Montana."

"I'm sure I would, but first I have a job to do."

"Well, do it and leave."

"I can't. You refuse to cooperate."

"If your job has anything to do with my mares, you're darn right I won't cooperate."

The laughter had disappeared from her voice.

"Then I can't leave. Not until I've convinced you that pasture breeding is superior to a cold injection."

Her face tensed. All the sleepy sweetness was gone. He wished he could get it back but he knew he'd stepped over the sweetness line.

"Fine, be obstinate."

"I will if you will."

"If I will what?"

"Be stubborn."

She was spitting mad now, he could tell…and she looked more adorable than ever…which only caused him more discomfort.

"Jake Scott, you drive me crazy."

He couldn't help the smile that seemed to come from somewhere deep within him. She sounded exactly like that little girl he'd fallen for all those years ago. "Kenzie Grant, I sometimes believe that's my whole purpose in life."

She let out a little throaty squeak, then abruptly disappeared inside and slammed the window shut so hard the lamp popped off the table and landed on the floor, shattering the bulb.

"Damn," he cussed as darkness encircled him.

"Thank you for putting out the light," she cooed through the closed window.

He didn't respond.

Chapter Three

Kenzie awoke to the smell of luscious, just-brewed coffee. It had somehow wafted into her bedroom and tickled her nose with its delightful, inviting aroma. It was the one scent she could bathe in for hours, the one taste she craved more than anything else in the morning.

Morning!

Kenzie bolted upright in her bed, realizing that the sun was already shining through her windows, which meant it had to be way past 5:00 a.m. When she glanced over at the clock and read nine thirty, she couldn't believe her eyes.

"What? That's impossible."

She slipped out of bed, and made a beeline to the bathroom down the hall where the bronze clock that hung next to the mirror echoed the same time.

"Darn!" she scolded out loud.

The night had not gone easy. She couldn't stop thinking about what she'd said to Jake about her making love like an alley cat…as if. What could have ever possessed her to say such a thing? She had no idea.

Sure, she'd slept with a few men over the years, but she could probably count them all on one hand. Okay, on three fingers. Kenzie wasn't exactly versed in the art of seduction when it came right down to it.

Still, that didn't seem to stop her competitive edge with respect to Jake Scott. She wanted him to see her as an all-around accomplished woman…even when it came to the bedroom. She only hoped it would never come to that, or she might possibly be in a heap of trouble.

Kenzie couldn't remember when she'd awoken so late. It had to have been back in her college days. Hopefully one of her hired cowboys had put the mares out or they'd be even twitchier than they already were.

She quickly showered; pulled her hair up in a ponytail; decided to apply eyeliner, mascara and lip gloss; dressed in her usual work attire of jeans and a T-shirt, checked a few things on her laptop and phone and then made her way into the kitchen. All she needed was a cup of that glorious-smelling coffee her mom had brewed and to wave goodbye to Jake as he drove away, and life on the ranch would settle back down…or as much as it could with her mares being in season and her parents' anniversary wedding moving up closer by the minute.

At this time of day, the kitchen would be virtually empty, and she looked forward to taking a moment to enjoy her first cup of coffee.

As she rounded the corner into the kitchen, not only did Dora and Dolly walk up to greet her, tails wagging, tongues flapping, but her mom sat at the table, along with her dad, her sister Callie, Callie's hubby, Joel Darwood, and the dreaded Jake Scott. He stood at the counter pouring coffee into a mug. And not just any old mug, but her favorite mug, the one she'd used almost every morning for the past five years, give or take a few weeks here and there when someone in the family would buy her a new one.

The fact that he hadn't left and had claimed her mug as his own when everyone around the table knew she'd brought that mug home from Paris when she'd gone there for a semester while she attended college was unbearable. His callous behavior, combined with her family's inability to stand up for her mug rights, caused her agitation…not to mention frustration that was quickly swelling to a bursting point.

And she was just about to blow off some steam when Jake held out the coveted mug. "Coffee?" he asked, looking all doe-like as he offered the mug that now contained her favorite brown liquid.

"Thanks," she mumbled trying her best to pull in her claws.

She smiled and swiped it from his hand. Then she padded over to the table where the pitcher of fresh milk sat and added a little to her brew.

Okay, so maybe he hadn't taken her mug, but he was still there, in the kitchen, when he should have been loading his stud horses into his trailer. Or better still, he should have been long gone with just his tire tracks left as a reminder of his short visit.

"Jake brought his own coffee beans and ground

them for us," Callie said, then she looked over at Jake and grinned.

"They're organic," her mom crooned, after she took a swig from her own special mug, the one she'd bought at Holy Rollers when they'd celebrated their first year in business…a bright pink mug with a picture of a crispy donut dripping with a white glaze and a halo floating over it. A pink box of donuts, muffins and scones lay open in the center of the table. Kenzie tried to ignore the box of goodies, but right away she spotted a raspberry scone, her absolute favorite breakfast food. Her mouth watered for the scone.

"Joel drove me into town and we stopped at a great bakery," Jake told Kenzie. "Wish we had something like that in Starlight Bend. Nothing even comes close. Amanda, the owner, told me you liked raspberry scones so I added a couple to the box."

"I'm not hungry this morning," Kenzie told him, even though her stomach growled for that yummy scone.

Every fiber of her being cried out, but she didn't want to give Jake the satisfaction of knowing he'd done something she clearly liked.

She wanted him gone…until she tasted the coffee. It was pure magic. The smooth flavors danced in her mouth and suddenly she couldn't stop lapping it up. She thought perhaps she'd let him stay long enough to brew another pot of the wondrous elixir, then he'd have to go for sure.

"I take it you like the coffee," Jake asked Kenzie,

looking all full of himself, as if *I told you so* would pop out of his mouth at any second.

She forced herself to put her mug down on the counter. "It'll do."

At this point, she had no choice but to lie through her teeth.

"It's the fresh cream," Jake said. "It really adds to the flavor."

"We stopped off at Bridget's Dairy Farm and bought a gallon of their milk from grass-fed cows," Joel offered, his baby blues twinkling. Kenzie really liked Joel…just not at the moment.

"There's so much cream in that there milk, it makes my coffee taste richer than one of your mom's cream pies," her dad added.

She felt as if everyone was ganging up on her, or at least tossing in their support of Jake Scott, the Troublemaker.

She wasn't in the mood this morning. She'd already checked the tracking number for her shipment of frozen semen and it hadn't even left Canada yet. It seemed to be stuck in customs for some reason. At this rate, she might miss the window of opportunity for her mares and have to wait until next month. That alone had put her in a sour mood, and now she had to deal with her family's praise for Jake's coffee, as if it was the end all of coffees.

And even if it was possibly the smoothest coffee she'd ever held on her tongue, did they have to fall all over him?

"It'll probably give me a heart attack before I'm thirty."

Kenzie said a short prayer asking for forgiveness to the coffee gods as she dumped the rest of her perfectly perfect coffee into the sink, then proceeded to make instant coffee with hot tap water. She knew everyone was watching her, thinking she was wacky, but she kept right on going. When she dumped in cold nonfat milk, she took a sip of the awful but familiar swill, made a yummy sound, and looked over at Jake. "I thought you were leaving this morning?"

He crooked an eyebrow, smirked and said, "Whatever gave you that idea?"

"You said so yourself last night."

He tilted his head, the grin never leaving his face and stared at her. "I don't recall ever saying I'd be leaving this morning. Not when your parents' anniversary is a little over a week away. I wouldn't dream of missing it."

"There's plenty of time for you to pack up, drive home and drive back down again, *without* your stud horses."

"Not really," Callie said as she grabbed the last raspberry scone from the box. Her dad had taken the other one. Kenzie's heart almost stopped. She wanted that scone in the worst way. Didn't her sister know that? Just because she was five months pregnant didn't mean she could go around taking other people's scones.

"Jake's agreed to help us go over our menu for the reception," her mom said, a wide grin on her lovely face. "He thinks we can actually save some money, and provide a healthier meal if we incorporate a few organic items."

"I already helped you with that menu, and we came up with some tasty side dishes. You said so yourself. It's too late to start messing with the menu now. We've already ordered some of the food."

"It's never too late to do the best thing for your guests," Jake mumbled while he poured another mug of coffee. This time he poured it into a travel mug she'd bought several years ago at the county fair: Keep Calm and Cowboy On.

She loved that travel mug.

"So," he said as he poured. "Joel, your dad and I trailed your mares out to the east pasture this morning, just in case you change your mind about my stallions."

He added cream to the mug, closed it up tight, smiled and held it out for Kenzie, the logo prominently on display.

She wanted to lay into him for moving her mares, but that dang Keep Calm and Cowboy On logo reminded her that anger was not how she should handle this situation. Obviously, not only was her dad on Jake's side, but so was her brother-in-law and her sister Callie. She wondered if even her own mother had fallen into the Jake-pit-of-cowboy-charm?

All she had to do at the moment was breathe…in, out…in, out.

"You might want this for later," he told her, the smirk gone, looking more sexy than a man had a right to. His dark hair had that tousled style she loved, and his once scruffy chin appeared to have been recently shaved. His green eyes sparkled, and his black T-shirt seemed extra tight across his muscled chest. If she didn't dislike his haughty attitude so much, she could see herself falling in step with this "natural" cowboy.

Just not today.

Not when he'd moved her mares without her consent. She vowed to never oversleep again, at least not until she could get him to leave…which she intended to do…today if possible.

This was war!

"I might," she answered, grabbing the dang travel mug from his outstretched hand, while she abandoned her own mug of bad-tasting tepid coffee on the counter. "Thanks."

Then she reached over and filched the raspberry scone off her sister's plate.

"You don't even like raspberries," she told Callie, as she hustled out of the back door with Jake trailing close behind.

AFTER A REALLY bad night's sleep due to a number of reasons, one of them being a complete lack of any sort of comfort, Jake thought things couldn't get much worse. But then what did he know about a woman who seemed to be on a mission to get him to leave as soon as possible?

He'd driven down to the Grant ranch to help out his dad's best friend, sure, but he had also hoped for some time to reflect and regroup. So far all of those desires seemed to be as elusive as a royal flush in a high-stakes poker game.

He'd gotten the okay from Henry that morning, while Kenzie slept, to move the mares out of the barn. Henry had assured him that it would be all right. The two hired hands were off that morning, so Jake had simply led the mares over. Joel helped out with the move, but he had his own ranch to run, the Double S, where Kenzie's parents' anniversary wedding ceremony would be held.

Jake had thought he and Joel were doing a good thing when the mares started getting restless in their stalls. They even cleaned the stalls while Kenzie slept, but none of that seemed to matter to her. Not even the fact that he'd made sure his stallions were secure in the corral before he and Joel walked the mares out to the fenced pasture.

Apparently, Kenzie didn't appreciate anything that they'd done.

"We have to move the mares back to the corral, and get your horses out of there. I would prefer you put them in your horse trailer and drive them back to Montana, but for now the barn is fine. That pasture is for my heifers. We're scheduled to move twenty-two heifers tomorrow morning."

"Then what's the harm in your mares spending today out there?"

She gazed at him while holding on to her mug, looking mighty good under the midmorning sun. He hoped she would agree because just getting the mares out into those pastures took a bit of doing. Like their owner, none of them were particularly cooperative.

"Fine," she finally said, "but they can't spend the night. The terrain might be too rugged for them in the dark."

"Then we'll bring them in before dusk."

"There's no *we* about it. You brought them out there, so you can lead them back. I'll be too busy with...other things to help you."

He thought by her hesitation that she was simply trying to make it more difficult on him. However, he liked that she wasn't pushing him off the ranch, either.

"Sounds like an invitation to stay another day."

She stared at him, took a long swallow from the travel mug and said, "I've got work to do. If you're going to be here anyway, maybe you can do something other than brew coffee and move my mares around."

"Whatever you need."

Her eyes went wide and he wondered what went on in that head of hers as she flashed a momentary smirk.

Then as soon as his gaze rested on her lips, the smile vanished. "You can help me clean out the guesthouse, load it all into my pickup and drive it over to my brother Carson's house in town. He's been too busy helping plan the upcoming Cowboy Days to get to it. That's where your parents will be staying once they arrive. I've been using it for storage and, I'm afraid, so have my siblings. It might be in pretty bad shape."

"If I help clean it out, would it be okay if I move in while I'm here?" As much as Jake liked being close to Kenzie at night, just knowing she made love like an alley cat didn't much help lull him to sleep…nor did the tiny size of the porch bed.

She squinted as they stood out in front of the horse barn, the sun blazing down on them like a spotlight in an interrogation room.

"Let me get this straight. Just how long do you intend to hang around here?"

"As long as it takes."

"As long as it takes for what?"

"For you to smile at me."

She flashed him a great big pearly white smile. "How's that?"

"Pathetic. My horse has a more genuine smile."

"Your horse doesn't know any better. You're the hand that feeds him."

"Is that what you want? Food? 'Cause if you do, I'm a great cook."

She stepped in closer to him, narrowing her eyes. "Is there anything you can't do, Jake Scott? Or are your virtues boundless?"

Teasing Kenzie had always been fun, but now that they were both adults, he had to admit, he liked it even more. His dad liked to tease his mom the same way. He always said it acted like a barometer. If his mom interacted with him, and got all riled up, he knew she still liked being with him. The day she stopped reacting was the day he'd start worrying.

So far, his dad didn't have a care in the world…

except maybe which of his sons would take over the ranch. Jake knew it would most likely be him, but for some reason, he hadn't really made that clear to his dad...yet. He didn't want to step on any toes in case one of his two brothers wanted the glory for himself. But so far, neither one had stepped up to the plate.

"Pretty much boundless," he told her, knowing it was total baloney. Lately, ever since his divorce, he couldn't seem to do the most menial of chores. He'd burn all his food, pound and poke his fingers whenever he'd try to mend a fence or build something. Forget to order hay and have to buy it locally paying almost twice the amount. The list was endless. He'd been so distracted with his own thoughts that whatever he tried to do wouldn't get done. Even his brothers had mentioned it to him, and Lucas had tried to pick up the slack.

And his parents...well, they just worried.

But since he'd gotten the phone call from Henry asking him to come on down for a spell, his whole attitude had begun to change.

And sparring with Kenzie seemed to pick up his spirits even more.

She threw him an eye roll. "You really are full of yourself, aren't you?"

"Just telling the truth."

"Oh, you always did infuriate me."

He thought about his dad's barometer and smirked. "And you always tempted me."

"What's that supposed to mean? Tempted you how?"

"To kiss you."

He leaned in, thinking maybe all her bluster was a prelude to that alley cat lover hidden inside, but she shoved him away with both hands, and he nearly fell right on his butt in the process.

"Let's get one thing straight. I'm only tolerating your presence here because my dad invited you. I have absolutely no desire to get intimate with you on any level. Do you understand me? Or is that pig-headed brain of yours too ripe with self-adulation that you can't understand the truth?"

That barometer was heading up toward the bursting point, and Jake loved every minute of it.

"I hear you loud and clear," he said, trying his best to avoid showing the smile that tugged at his lips. "Now, where's that guest cabin?"

THE CABIN WAS in worse shape than Kenzie had envisioned it to be. Not only was it filled with Carson's things, but some of the furniture had water damage from an apparent open window and the wooden floor in front of the window had warped.

Carson had not only stored boxes inside the cabin, but it seemed as if it had turned into a catchall for everyone in the family except Kenzie. The front door had to be shoved open, which Kenzie managed to do without Jake's help, thank you very much, and some of the windows were swollen shut.

Jake had to open those, but only after Kenzie had loosened them with brute force, at least that was what she told herself.

Plus, some animal must have died in there because the whole place reeked.

"And my parents are going to stay…where?" Jake waved a hand in front of his face, trying to get the smell to dissipate.

"Here," she said, hopeful they could get it cleared out in time.

"Maybe a nice motel in town might be better."

"Not an option. Along with guests from Joel's family, and from our extended family, both inns are booked and the one motel that's within easy driving distance has an Idaho potato convention going on that weekend. We have no choice but to get this cabin cleaned out pronto."

"Seems impossible."

"That's where you and I differ. I look at it as a challenge to overcome, while you look at it as an insurmountable obstacle. Seems you still suffer from a lack of imagination."

She knew that Jake hated to admit she was completely right on that point. He never could dream like she could, never could imagine himself anywhere else but working his family ranch, and with a few exceptions, most likely in the exact same way it had been worked for generations.

Kenzie on the other hand had *chosen* to run her family ranch. She'd had the grades to do almost anything else she'd put her mind to, but ranching had always been her passion…and maybe being a ballerina, or for a short time, a priest, like her cousin Father Beau, who was going to perform the ceremony for

her parents at Saint Paul's Catholic Church in town.
The church where her siblings had gotten married,
and where she might one day do the same.

But most definitely not to Jake Scott, even though
that vision had crossed her mind several times while
she was growing up...at least until he kissed her and
laughed. After that, she'd pushed that stupid thought
right out of her head.

Until now.

"You might be right about that," he said.

"What? Did I hear you correctly? Did you say I
might be right?"

"About my imagination, yes? About all your chemicals, no."

Jake made a beeline past several clear plastic con-
tainers neatly stacked until he came to cardboard
boxes filled with preservatives for hay.

"You don't actually use this stuff?"

She didn't like his tone.

"Sometimes. When we cut our hay and it's too
wet to bale."

"It's not good for your animals to eat this junk."

"There's no evidence to support that, and it keeps
our hay from molding or, worse, from generating too
much heat once it's baled."

"Wait until it's not raining to cut it down, usually
late morning, and give it a day or two to dry before
you bale it."

"We used to do that, and we ended up with a lot
more mold and had to destroy the bales. Plus, we don't
always have the time for that."

"You just aren't doing it right. I can show you exactly what you need to do."

"Will it save me time and money?"

"In the long run, it should. Yes."

"Have you crunched the numbers like I have?"

"Ranching isn't just about dollars and cents. It's about the all-around health of your land, your crops and your livestock. You can't put a price tag on those kinds of things."

She knew he was right, but that kind of thinking had almost brought this ranch into bankruptcy. Something had had to change, and she'd made those changes, even at the cost of using a few chemicals to speed things up.

"How many acres do you have?" she asked, knowing perfectly well the Scott ranch was much larger than the Grant ranch.

"Just over sixty thousand."

"We have just under four thousand, and most of it is too rugged to use. We can't afford to lose any hay to mold, or bugs, or what have you, and we can't afford for any of our heifers, cows or mares to go barren for a season. That's the reality of a small ranch like ours. Now, if you want to help, you can carry these boxes out to my truck. Anything else, like your opinion on my ranching style, is best left unsaid. Or you can load up your trailer and drive on out of here right this minute, despite what my dad says."

She knew there was absolutely no way he would leave, especially now that he knew what she was adding to the hay. He'd be even more determined than ever to prove to her that there were more natural methods to do things that were just as effective, and all around much better for both the animals and for the handlers.

But she didn't care. Ranching these days was all about the bottom line, and right now, the Grant ranch had a profitable bottom line, and that was all that mattered.

"I've been invited down here by a man I respect and my family respects a great deal. He's asked me to help turn this ranch back to a more natural state without stepping on your toes. If I have to tread a little lighter then so be it, but I don't intend to disappoint him by leaving just because you and I can't seem to come to terms."

"I assume it's until my parents renew their vows. Am I right?"

"Yes. I have a roundup to get back to. My brother Curt is still in Portland and Lucas depends on me to head up our team of hired wranglers, so I'll be heading back the next day, along with everyone else in my family."

Kenzie shook her head as she tried to ease the tension that was building behind her eyes.

"My dad is a smart man, but on this issue, he's just wrong and so are you."

"I'm not going to stop giving you suggestions. It's what I was asked to do."

"And I'm not going to start listening. Modern commercial ranching is what I was trained to do, and what I believe in. It's also the only solution to keep this ranch lucrative."

She knew a lot of small ranchers who felt exactly like she did. Some of them had made it, but the majority of them had eventually converted over to a combination of natural and commercial means. Jake apparently leaned more on the natural side, so he wouldn't understand the middle-of-the-road approach, and if he did, she felt certain he wouldn't admit it…especially not at the moment.

"And is it working so far?"

"Yes, it's moved us away from having to file for bankruptcy."

"I had no idea the Grant ranch had come that close. Neither had my dad. Henry never mentioned it. I get why you're so adamant about your methods. I know that kind of fear. Every rancher does. My family ranch means everything to me, as I'm sure it does to you and your family. Or why else would you be fighting me so hard?"

For the first time since he'd arrived, Kenzie felt as if he understood some of what she'd been going through, but it still didn't justify his arrogance about natural ranching.

"Because my methods work for this ranch."

"Then we've reached an understanding of sorts," he told her, sounding almost reasonable.

"How do you figure? Seems to me we've reached an impasse."

It was never going to work out between them. She felt certain about it now.

"Not really. What we've done is we've agreed to disagree. So the way I see it, we only have one recourse."

She threw him a sly little smile. "For you to leave?"

But she knew he wouldn't be willing to pack it in just yet.

"No. I won't do that, but we can try to do our best to convince one another that each of our ways of ranching is the best way. I mean, I don't know squat about commercial ranching."

She knew that wasn't true. He was too smart to be that dumb. She'd bet the ranch that he knew quite a bit about it from neighboring ranchers, but maybe he'd be willing to give her methods a fresh look.

He continued, "And from what I can tell, you know about as much about natural or organic ranching. Maybe for the next couple of weeks, we could each try to learn from each other. I'm willing to have an open mind if you are."

He held out his hand as a gesture.

She gazed down at it as if he was asking her to take hold of the wrong end of a branding iron. Her forehead furrowed, and a skeptical grimace was about all she could muster.

"I don't know if I can," she said. "I've worked so hard to get the ranch where it is today that I would feel like I'm taking a step back."

"All I'm asking for is an open mind. If this old cowboy who's set in his ways can do it, certainly you can at least try…for your dad's sake, if nothing else. And it's only for a few days. It's not like you have to commit to anything. All you have to do is listen. You'd make your dad happy. What do ya say?"

She could tell he was laying it on thick. And if truth be told, she knew he meant it…maybe not completely, but he seemed willing to try if she was.

"I can't promise I won't fight you on every suggestion."

"I would expect nothing less. Besides, I intend to fight you on your suggestions, but I'll still listen to what you have to say."

Her shoulders slackened a bit. She shuffled her feet and reluctantly stuck out her hand.

As soon as she touched his skin, a warm sensation swept through her. His face told her he'd felt it, as well. Suddenly all the arguing seemed unimportant, all their differences floated away. She didn't quite understand what was happening. Why she wanted him to take her in his arms. Why she wanted to start over and take the time to get to know him better. To try to figure him out.

"Kenzie, I—"

But she slipped her hand out of his grasp before he could finish his sentence.

"I'll empty this room, if you'll take the bedrooms," she said. "I'd like to drive into town early before the shops close. I've got to stop at the hardware store for some supplies, if that's okay with you."

She could feel the flush on her face, on her skin, and hoped he didn't notice. Something had happened between them, but she didn't want to pursue it, and he seemed willing to back down, as well.

"Anything you want to do is fine by me," he said, and she could tell he meant it.

Chapter Four

"You know you didn't have to do this," Carson repeated to Kenzie for the third time. "I had every intention of picking up my stuff this weekend."

He'd been using that same stale line for the past several months.

"I couldn't take the chance, dear brother," Kenzie told him as Jake slipped the last box into the storage shed in Carson's backyard. The three of them had made several trips back and forth to Kenzie's pickup to collect everything, and now Kenzie and Carson stood just outside waiting for Jake to secure the last of the load.

Carson and his wife, Zoe, still lived in the small rental they'd taken before they were married. Zoe's wedding planning business, We Do I Do's, had an office in town inside the bridal shop, All About the Bride, and she and Carson had decided that living only a few blocks away was a lot easier for her than living twenty minutes away on the ranch, especially during the winter months. "Besides, now that Jake is staying for a couple weeks, he needs a place to sleep."

Carson turned to her while Jake rearranged a few of the boxes inside the large metal shed. Married life agreed with her brother. Now in his early thirties, he looked more content, and he'd just gone an entire year without a broken bone, a cracked rib, a dislocated shoulder or a torn muscle of any kind. Although he'd won the Nationals for bronc riding, and the town and his family were proud of him, it was nice to know that part of his life was over, and had been replaced with teaching young riders.

"No reason why he can't take my old room," he told Kenzie. "I haven't used it for any length of time in years."

Kenzie didn't want Jake sleeping in Carson's room. It was right next to hers, so no real improvement over Jake sleeping on the porch, and well, she wanted him as far away from her as possible. Ever since that handshake she felt different toward him and wanted him to keep his distance. It was bad enough that they'd had to ride to town together…in the same truck…sitting next to each other…breathing the same air.

She hated that she was attracted to him when he stood for everything she was opposed to, everything she didn't want in a man, starting with the fact that he lived in Montana. Not that she would ever even consider Jake as anything but a pain in the neck, but if by chance she did let her guard down, she would never leave the Grant ranch. It was where she intended to raise her kids. Precisely the reason she fought so hard to keep it.

The Grant ranch was her future, her family's future, and no matter what kind of sparks flew between herself and Jake Scott, no matter how warm she felt holding his hand, nothing was going to pry her off the ranch she loved.

Her mind raced for a logical reason why Jake couldn't sleep in Carson's room. When she finally settled on one, she felt proud of herself for having the presence of mind to think on her feet...something she'd always been good at.

"You know perfectly well your room isn't fixed up for guests. You still have your posters glued up on the ceiling and on the walls. Some of your clothes from when you were in high school are still in the drawers. Your stuff is everywhere, and besides, Mom's been using it for a sewing room." The sewing room part was a complete fabrication, but she was desperate.

"Since when?" Carson accused.

"Since last month when we all bought her that new sewing machine for her birthday."

Carson couldn't argue with that. They'd all pitched in and surprised her, but so far, she hadn't even taken it out of the box. She'd been too busy working with Zoe planning her anniversary gala to try to learn all the bells and whistles on that sewing machine. For now, she was still using her old machine that was set up in the laundry room.

Fortunately, Carson didn't know that.

"Do you need any more help setting up the cabin for Jake's family? I might be able to give you a couple hours tomorrow after we move those heifers to the open pasture. I won't have to be at the riding school until around noon. My class doesn't start until twelve thirty."

Carson taught several different classes on horseback riding over at M&M Riding School four days a week on top of helping out on the family ranch whenever Kenzie really needed him. Plus, with all the work he had to do for the Cowboy Days next week, she knew his time was limited. Still, she didn't think she could take care of everything before her mom and dad renewed their marriage vows, a week from Saturday.

"Well, someone left a window open in the living room, and the floor under the window can probably use some work."

Not only was Carson a world-class National Rodeo Champion, a certified riding instructor and an all-around great brother (most of the time), he was also a talented craftsman. He could repair just about anything, including a warped wooden floor.

"I'll bring my tools and have a look."

"Thanks," she told him just as Jake emerged from the storage bin, a thin layer of sweat glistening on his forehead. He'd left his hat inside the cab of the truck, and his dark hair only accentuated those emerald eyes of his. He wiped his forehead on his arm in a manly gesture that reminded Kenzie that she really needed to get away from him, needed to get back to the ranch where she could isolate herself from him by doing some bookkeeping, or bedding down the stalls, or checking on the cows or doing any number of tasks to keep him off her mind.

"I believe that's it. I emptied everything out of

the truck. Hope you didn't mind my moving some of those boxes around inside there, but I needed a little more room."

"Not a problem. Sure you don't want another beer?"

Both Carson and Jake had already downed a beer each. Even though the temperature wasn't up in the eighties, the sun had been brutal, and even Kenzie had gone for a cold one along with a tall glass of water.

"No thanks. One will do me for now." He turned to Kenzie. "I'll swing that tailgate back up and wait for you in the truck."

Jake made his way back, as Kenzie said, "Well, we better get going. I've got to pick up some things in town, and Jake has to bring the mares in from the pasture."

Carson seemed to bristle at her words.

"Seems like your hired hands can do that. Last I heard, Jake is a guest."

Kenzie hated when her brother, or any of her siblings, second-guessed her authority on ranch duties. They'd all agreed the ranch was hers to run as she saw fit, and now it seemed that everyone, including Carson, was questioning that decision.

She wasn't in the mood for Carson's opinion, not after she and Jake just unloaded about thirty of *his* boxes.

"He brought my mares out there, he can bring them back," Kenzie said, using a decisive voice.

"According to Joel, the two of them led your mares

out because you were sleeping, and Jake needed somewhere to keep his stallions…which I hear are mighty fine quarter horses. Aren't his stallions in the corral now?"

"They are, but let's not get into this, Carson. It's not your concern."

"I don't mind," Jake added. "We should've waited for Kenzie, but your dad gave us the go-ahead so we acted on good faith. But now I realize we should have waited. It was Kenzie's call, not your dad's."

"The way I see it, you did her a favor. She should be grateful and treat you more like a guest, rather than one of her employees. But then as I remember it, you two always did have a prickly relationship." He glanced over at Kenzie and shook his head as if there was no hope.

"We're working through that," she said.

"Sure you are," Carson answered with a sarcastic tone, then he proceeded to lock up his shed.

She stepped up closer to her brother, so she could look him straight in the eye like she always did whenever she wanted to stand up for herself.

"Jake is not a guest. Dad asked him to come down and tell me how to ranch. I resent Dad for doing that, and I resent Jake for agreeing to it. So with that in mind, maybe you should stay out of this, big brother, unless you're somehow involved and no one has bothered to tell me."

He didn't respond so she backed down and was about to leave when Carson said, "Well, since you put it like that, you should know that I might have suggested to Dad that he contact Jake, but I never thought he'd actually do it or that Jake would show up."

"You're kidding, right?"

He shrugged, then hightailed it back inside the house before Kenzie could give him a piece of her mind.

After that, all bets were off.

THERE WERE SEVERAL times when Kenzie and Jake were inside From the Ground Up, the local hardware store, that Jake had wanted to speak up. He'd wanted to inform Kenzie about a better product than the one she tossed into her cart. He knew for a fact that a certain gage wire or a certain type of hinge was more effective than what she had chosen, but based on how she wheeled her cart around, almost as if it were a weapon, combined with the scowl on her face, Jake decided that any suggestions he might have might very well bring the roof down on both their heads.

So instead, he merely went along with everything she bought or said...not that she said very much. Whenever she spoke it was more to herself rather than to him, but he didn't care. He understood her anger and frustration, he just didn't like that it was mainly directed at him.

After they loaded everything in the bed of the truck, then secured it with a tarp and rope, they headed out of town. Aside from the short trip to Holy Rollers that morning, it had been a while since Jake had been to Briggs and as he drove past some of the more colorful shops, he marveled at how well kept the storefronts were. Also, how many people milled around.

Dusk had settled in the Teton Valley, and the sky was awash with color that edged the billowy clouds as they floated in perfect formation toward the majestic mountains. By now, almost seven thirty on a weeknight, his town sometimes looked so deserted a stranger might think no one lived there.

But Briggs was a vibrant town, one that had added a few features to make it stand out. Like the large plaster spud perched on the roof of Spud Bank, or the life-sized dairy cow, complete with pink udders, greeting the patrons of Moo's Creamery, which was doing a grand business on this balmy night. Then there was Deli Llama's with its own version of a very large llama out front. He'd noticed most of the shops that morning when he'd driven in with Joel, but they'd been so busy talking that he hadn't gotten the chance to really check out all the endearing aspects of the place. For instance, he hadn't noticed the tavern at the edge of town until they stopped for the red light directly in front of it.

Belly Up seemed like the kind of tavern a man could ease into for the night and not feel guilty about it in the morning. Through the plate glass windows out front, he could tell that Belly Up was one of those neighborhood taverns where Christmas parties and birthday celebrations were held. He wanted to be a part of that scene. It had been a long, hard day, and the way he had it figured, they could both use a respite and sit a spell. Only problem was he thought for sure that trying to convince Kenzie to stop in would be like trying to bathe a wild coyote.

"Want to grab a beer? I'm buying," Jake said as they idled in front of the tavern.

They hadn't really spoken to each other since they left her brother's house, so he thought he'd try something simple. Something that only required a yes or no answer.

"If you're buying, I'm drinking," she said, surprising the heck out of him, as she immediately swung the pickup to the curb, shoved the transmission into Park, pulled out the key and then jumped out before he could wrap his mind around her quick response.

Kenzie Grant had actually agreed to something he'd suggested. Perhaps he should have tried it in the hardware store…or not.

He followed her inside, enjoying the ambience of a real honky-tonk, with its wooden floor, pounding country music and mile-long mahogany bar that skirted an entire wall. A single mirror, the likes of which he'd never seen before, ran behind the polished wooden bar displaying various liquors, wines and glistening glassware.

He watched as Kenzie nodded and greeted more than half the patrons as she made her way to an empty table in the back. A large painting of a seminude woman lying on a chaise hung on the wall. Kenzie took a seat at a square table and he did the same, sitting across from her, wondering if they would actually have a conversation or would she continue with her silent treatment?

"This place is great," he began, hoping she'd eventually relax. "Seems like just the place to kick up your boots after a long day or week. You come here often?"

"Not enough, according to my family. First time in months."

"I'm honored."

She threw him the tiniest of grins and his entire world lit up. "Don't be. It was merely time, that's all."

"Whatever it takes."

"A lot, believe me. There are so many things I could be doing right now," she said, while nodding over at one of two bartenders. Jake immediately got the impression the two women knew each other.

"Everyone takes a day off to rest," he said.

Another tiny smile. He was batting a thousand.

"You made your point," she said, and for the first time since he'd been on the ranch, she seemed to throw off some of the tension that consumed her 24/7.

"As I live and breathe…Miss Kenzie Grant," the bartender, a petite twentysomething woman, crooned as she approached the table. She was dressed entirely in black, including a logo T-shirt tucked into her tight-fitting jeans. "Well, get out, girlfriend! I haven't seen you in this bar since your sister Callie's bachelorette party, and that had to be a couple months ago."

"Almost four," Kenzie said, as a bright smile lit up her face. It was nice to see a full-out smile even if it wasn't directed at him. Jake was beginning to think she'd never truly smile again…at least not while he was in her company.

"Wow, that's too long, babe. You really need to get

out more. But you're here now, and that's all that matters." She turned to Jake, giving him a big warm grin as her intense gaze quickly tumbled over his face, chest and arms. "And who's this handsome cowboy? New to Briggs or just passing through?"

Jake stood and held out a hand as Kenzie did the introductions. "Sophie Coontz is one of Belly Up's incredible new bartenders. Sophie, this is a friend of the family, Jake Scott. He's here for my parents' anniversary party next week. He's also been helping out on the ranch."

Stunned that Kenzie would admit that bit of information, Jake's reaction time lagged as he and Sophie exchanged smiles and a friendly handshake. After everything Kenzie had told him about not wanting his assistance, there she was announcing it to a friend.

"So you're the reason why she's in here tonight. Maybe you can stay awhile and give her more free time. With five kids of my own, I'd sure love some. This lady's nonstop. Glad to meet the man who gave her a break."

"Wait a minute. Did you say five kids?" Jake had a hard time wrapping his mind around that. Two kids was a handful, but five?

"Yes, and I'm three months pregnant with my sixth, another girl. That makes three of each," she chuckled.

"You're pregnant?" Kenzie jumped up and gave Sophie a hug across the bar. "Oh, sweetie, that's fabulous news!"

The two women talked and chortled while Jake

tried to imagine how this woman juggled five young children, a job and a burgeoning pregnancy. Just one child had been a point of contention between himself and his ex-wife…a *big* point of contention.

When the excitement died down, Sophie took their drink order for two beers and went off to fetch them.

"Wow, five kids. I can't even imagine," he said out loud more to himself than to Kenzie.

"I come from a family of five kids, remember?"

"Yeah, but that was more the norm back then."

"Oh, yeah, back in the good old days when sliced bread was just invented. What are you talking about? Five kids was never the norm, two or three maybe, but five? Sophie's amazing. She'll probably have a few more before she and Liam are finished. What about you? Ever think about having kids?"

He liked how Kenzie could cut to the heart of the matter, even when she wasn't aware of what she was doing.

"All the time," he said, not really wanting to get into it. "What about you?"

"Oh, no you don't. You're not putting that loaded question back on me without really answering it yourself."

He moved his napkin to a closer spot on the table, whishing there was a cold beer sitting on it. "I don't know if this is the right place to get into it, but yeah, I've thought about having a family of my own lots of times. I'm sure you know I was married for a short while. Didn't last long. Funny how before you're married you both agree on everything, then once reality sets in, all those agreements seem to fly out the window. Been divorced a little over ten months now. The wound is still a little raw."

"It must have been comforting to be able to talk about it with your brothers. I know my sisters and I can always talk about everything. And Carson, well, he's my hero when it comes to advice. The guy's better than a psychologist…at least he is usually."

Jake shook his head. He wished he could talk to his brothers about personal stuff, but he couldn't. "I haven't talked to anyone about it, and truth be told, it's eating me up inside, especially since my mom loved my ex like the daughter she never had."

"But what about your brothers? Wasn't Lucas engaged once? He seems like the right person to talk to."

"Lucas was engaged for all of three days before she dumped him and moved to Denver, where she's a CEO of some big company now. But that's beside the point. I've never been that close to my brothers. Always thought that since they're less than a year apart, they acted like twins. Mom even dressed them alike until they were almost six, and only stopped when they started first grade. Our dad put an end to Mom's obsession with their clothes. He went out and bought Lucas a whole new wardrobe for first grade. It wasn't even remotely anything like Curt's clothes for kindergarten."

"But whenever we visited, you three were always together."

"Believe me, it wasn't by choice. My mom forced them to watch me while she was off doing her chores around the ranch. They hated it, and resented me for holding them down. Not that they were mean or anything like that. My brothers treated me well, they just didn't always want me around, and I could tell."

"And here I thought you were the bully of the family."

He softly chuckled remembering some of his more aggressive behavior as a kid. He was a handful even for his brothers.

"I believe they call that 'acting out.' I'm a full four years younger than Lucas and Curt. Besides, Curt's been off finding himself for the last three years, so he certainly doesn't have time to help define my emotions while he's searching for his own."

She glanced around the room, fidgeting with her own napkin, then looked right into his eyes. "I'm sorry. I didn't mean to bring up, I mean...I just thought... Actually, I don't know what I thought. If you don't want to talk about it, we don't have to. I'm often too blunt and intrusive. I don't mean to be. It's just that I'm not much for small talk and would rather talk about the important stuff. But I understand if I hit a nerve."

"It's okay. I'm getting better with it now. At first I was stunned when Heather—that's her name—walked out, especially since she never gave me a chance to fix what was broken. I've always been good at fixing things...apparently not so much with matters of the heart."

Sophie returned with the beers, and two glasses of water. Jake drank down half of the pint of beer before he put his glass down while Kenzie took a few sips, then guzzled her water.

When she put the glass back down, she asked the question Jake had been avidly avoiding for the past year. "What broke, if you don't mind my asking?"

He sucked in a deep breath then slowly let it out. Of all the people he thought he could bare his soul to, Kenzie Grant had never been on his list...until now.

"Our love affair broke. It shattered into a million pieces when she told me she'd decided she never wanted kids. We'd talked about it before we were married, and I knew she was cool to the idea, but I always thought that would change once we were married. It changed all right. She'd gotten an accounting job with a big fracking company and after only a few months, they offered her a position where she'd have to travel the country for more than half the month. She took it without even talking it over with me. That's when she decided that for the foreseeable future, she didn't want any children, and when I pressed her, that foreseeable future stretched out to her retirement."

"A lot of women put their careers first. There's nothing wrong with that."

"Of course not, and I'm all for it, but she married a rancher who wanted kids."

"And you expected her to fall into ranching alongside you, is that it? And when she didn't, you probably shut down."

"Major shutdown, especially when she started traveling. I couldn't get past it." He leaned in closer. "So

tell me. You work twenty-four-seven on your ranch.
What would you have done if your new husband had
taken a job that meant he was almost never home, and
told you he didn't want any children…ever?"

"I wouldn't have married him in the first place. I
loved growing up with all my siblings. Never a dull
moment, plus I always had someone to play with and
talk to. I can only marry a rancher who loves kids.
No one else will do."

He suddenly wished he had met up with Kenzie
years ago, before he'd got tangled up with his ex.
Maybe things would have been different…a lot different.

"But what if you didn't know your guy didn't want
kids and didn't want any part of ranching before you
were married? What if he never really told you the
truth?"

"That wouldn't happen. Not to me. I'm careful
about who I fall in love with…not that I've ever really been in love."

"Never?"

"I don't think so."

"Believe me, you know when you're in love. You
don't have to think about it, you just are. So what if
it did happen? What if Mr. Right wasn't truthful with
you until after the wedding?"

She sat there and took another couple sips of beer,
then said, "Even if it ripped out my heart, I'd walk
away. Ranching means too much to me…my family
ranch means too much to me. I could never share it

with someone who didn't feel the same, or with someone who didn't want to raise our kids on the ranch."

"You said 'kids.' Does that mean you want more than one?"

"At least four. Always wanted four kids, and two dogs. There's a piece of land on the ranch, right on the other side of those pastures you saw today. It's on high ground, looks out over the entire ranch and has a clear view of the mountains. Someday I'm going to build a house right there."

"What if the guy you fall in love with doesn't want to live there? What if he…what if he has his own ranch somewhere else? What would you do?"

She stared at him and he wondered if she caught what he was saying. Not that he was in love with her, but that, as crazy as it seemed, he had feelings for her.

"I would try not to fall in love with him," she said in a low, soft voice, as if she was sorry about her answer.

"Haven't you heard that old saying: 'You don't choose love. Love chooses you'?"

She took a sip of beer, looked around, as a sly grin creased her lips. "Is that what happened to you? Love chose you?"

"It did, at least for a while. But you're not answering my question. What would you do if he had a ranch somewhere else? Would you leave your ranch for his?"

"I'd—" But before Kenzie could answer, her phone rang. Within moments her lighthearted demeanor changed as she listened, then clicked off the call.

"That was Coco," she said, as she stood and fished a few dollars out of her pocket. "We have to go. Sweet Girl, my horse, had an accident out in the pasture."

"SHE'S SKINNED UP her left fore cannon bone," Coco said while she, Jake and Kenzie stood in the well-lit barn next to Sweet Girl's stall. A cool night had descended on the valley, and Kenzie felt its chill. "She's walking fine, but Chad, one of your high school volunteers, called with concern when he brought her in for the night, so I drove over to check it out. The good thing is there are no broken or chipped bones. Sweet Girl should be fine in a couple days. Just stall her and hose the wound every few hours for the next day or two."

It was all Kenzie could do to keep her emotions in check. Eventually almost every horse on the ranch would get a scrape or two or injure some part of their bodies. It was just part of daily life, but Sweet Girl was her baby and she hated to see her in any kind of pain.

"Did you give her anything?"

"Yes, for the pain and inflammation." Coco put an arm around Kenzie's shoulders, and brought her in close. "Chad caught it in time. He's one fine young cowboy. You're lucky to have him. There's nothing for you to worry about."

Jake nuzzled up to Sweet Girl as she hung her head over the half door, giving her some much needed loving.

Kenzie wanted to blame him for bringing the

mares out to pasture in the first place, but she knew it wasn't really his fault. Accidents happened no matter how hard you tried to avoid them.

"I'll sleep in here for the night so I can run a hose on Sweet Girl's leg every couple of hours."

"I can stay out here, as well. We can do it in shifts."

Kenzie didn't really want to agree to this, but she knew it was the best thing for her horse. "Fine. There's plenty of room up in the loft for both of us."

Coco gave her a look. "We still have that old bed out here? I thought Dad got rid of that years ago when he caught Kayla in the loft with one of the Granger brothers."

Except it wasn't Kayla. Kenzie thought back to that moment as if it was yesterday. She had come back to the ranch with some of her friends, and one thing led to another and before she knew it she was kissing a Granger brother, an experience she wouldn't trade for anything. It was perhaps the best kiss of her teen years or for that matter, ever.

"The bed is gone, but I redid the space up there with fireproof flooring, so it's all new. Plenty of room for two people to sleep on the hay with some blankets. And for your information, that was me with a Granger brother, and we weren't 'out here,' at least not like that. We were just kissing."

Coco's face softened as if she had a memory of her own. "Which brother?"

"The youngest. Travis."

A wide sly grin slowly spread on Coco's lips.

"Did I ever tell you that I kissed Colt Granger once at Skaits ice-skating pond?"

"No, you did not. How could you not have told me that? It's one of those important sisterly bonding things."

"It was during that time when you'd sworn off kissing boys. I remember thinking it might not be a good idea to tell you about how I turned into mush when Colt took me in his arms and kissed me. That boy almost ruined it for me. I used to compare every other boy's kiss to Colt's kiss. Truth be told, he still holds the record for best kiss."

"Travis did the same for me, only in a different way." She turned and glared at Jake. "Travis restored my confidence." She could tell Jake was pretending not to hear any of this, so she gave him a little nudge.

"What?" he asked trying his best to look as if he had no idea what she was referring to, but Kenzie wasn't buying his feigned bewilderment.

"Oh, don't go playing all innocent with me. You know perfectly well what you did," she accused.

"Hey, I don't want to know what either of you did," Coco said handing Kenzie a couple of extra-large white tubes of some sort of ointment. "Rub this on the area after you hose off Sweet Girl's leg. She'll need it applied four times a day, and like I said, keep her stalled for at least forty-eight hours. Now, I've got to go. Been a long day."

They hugged and Kenzie felt grateful that her sister was such a great vet, and always available for whatever injury or illness that arose on the ranch.

Kenzie really didn't know how she could do it without her. "Thanks. I know Sweet Girl will be fine now. Love you, babe."

Coco returned her love and said her goodbyes then walked out of the barn, leaving Kenzie and Jake alone.

"Okay, so what did I do?"

"Oh, don't give me that. You know exactly what you did."

Kenzie marched out of the barn and headed to her truck, with Jake dogging her every step. She kept a blanket rolled up in the back of the cab for emergencies. This was an emergency. If she went looking for comforts inside the house, one of her parents would try to talk her out of sleeping in the barn, and she didn't want to get into it with them.

Not now. Not when Sweet Girl needed her.

"What? When?" Jake asked, his voice booming from behind her.

"When I was sixteen. You kissed me, and don't even tell me you don't remember, because it was the first thing you mentioned when you arrived."

She opened the cab door, grabbed the red wool blanket, slammed the door shut and headed back to the barn aware of the moonlight guiding her, the gentle breeze pushing through the trees and the sounds of cattle bellowing softly in the distance as they welcomed the long night. She was surrounded by everything she truly loved, except for Jake Scott.

He was the fly in the ointment of her discontent.

"Oh, *that* kiss," he said, but she knew he had no idea how his laughter had effected her.

"You really don't get it, do you?"

For months after that disheartening kiss, she'd stressed and fussed over what she might have done wrong. And not only that, she couldn't even kiss another boy for an entire year. It wasn't until her friends had convinced Travis Granger to kiss her that she'd finally gotten over her fear. And she wouldn't have done it then if it hadn't been one of the Granger brothers. Every girl for a hundred miles knew that the Granger brothers could make a girl's toes curl with just one kiss.

She couldn't pass that up, no matter how badly she might kiss him back.

Travis didn't laugh, not even when she went in for a second and third kiss. Her dad had come in and caught them just as they were about to kiss once again. She'd gotten grounded after that, for two solid weeks. That stopped any momentum she and Travis might have had. Besides, he was always pining over Bella Biondi anyway, so no other girl in town ever stood a chance with him. But still, Kenzie always had a fondness for Travis Granger.

Unlike her distaste for Jake Scott…which, the more she thought about that embarrassing kiss, was actively returning.

"Wait, you're talking about that awkward kiss we shared when the lights went off during Mariam Weiner's birthday party when you were sixteen, right?"

They arrived back in the barn and faced each other.

He truly looked perplexed. As if he was trying to remember what could have possibly gone wrong. He removed his hat and raked his hair straight back, causing him to look impossibly striking.

"Yes. I'd been following you around all night because I felt completely out of place. Everyone was a lot older than me. Then when the lights went out, you turned and kissed me…and laughed."

"I'm sorry, but I never expected you to kiss me back. I thought you'd push me away, like you always did whenever I got too close, but when you didn't, well…" He shrugged. "I was just coming off one of the worst colds I'd ever had, and my nose wouldn't stop itching. My mom had given me cough syrup before I left for that party and I was feeling a little woozy. Wait, I didn't attempt anything else, did I? Because if I did, I—"

"What? No. Wasn't that bad enough?"

He stared straight into her eyes, a smile tugging at his lips. "That I kissed you?"

"That you laughed. I felt humiliated."

"Wow, I had no idea. Is that why you've been so angry with me for all these years? Why you stopped coming out to Montana with your folks? Why you were never around when we drove out here? Why you don't like me telling you about natural ranching? Because I laughed during something really unexpected while I was dizzy on cough syrup?"

"I was traumatized, afraid to kiss another boy for a long time."

"If I remember correctly, I didn't *laugh* laugh. It

was more of a snicker or chuckle. Did you ever think that maybe I was a little shocked, and didn't know how to handle it?"

"Is that your excuse? You were shocked?"

A wide grin graced his lips, his eyes sparkled as he stretched his arms out wide trying to reach her. "Yeah. I was, so come on over here and let's try that kiss again. I promise I won't be laughing this time."

For a moment, she wanted to do just that, fall into his arms and kiss him like he'd never been kissed before.

But she didn't.

Instead, she stepped back. "You can't be serious. I just bared my soul to you and you want to kiss me?"

She headed for the loft, taking each stair with a heavy thud of her boots. He followed.

"Darlin', with words like that there's a lot more that I'd like to do than just kiss you."

When they arrived at the top of the stairs and entered the loft, she turned back to him.

"Do you even know how infuriating you are?"

"So I've been told," he said, but it was too late. Whatever shred of affection she'd felt had completely vanished. Instead, she tossed her blanket on the hay, dropped down and rolled herself up like a burrito.

"If you're staying, you'll have to get your own dang blanket, 'cause you can't use mine," she told him as he lay down next to her.

"Don't need one. Just lying next to you will generate enough heat to keep me warm."

And with that, Kenzie reached up and turned out the barn lights on the wall next to her.

"Don't even think about touching me," she told him while her eyes adjusted to the dark.

"I can't promise the not thinking part, but I set my phone to ring in two hours. I'll hose down Sweet Girl the first time so you can get some rest."

"Thanks," she said as her eyelids began to flutter. "I'll take the next shift. And stay on your own side."

"I'll do my best," she heard him say just before she blissfully drifted off to sleep.

Chapter Five

Kenzie slowly emerged from a luscious dream where she and Jake Scott had been riding Sweet Girl bareback while he held her close from behind. She leaned back into him, feeling the warmth of the sun on her body, and his strong arms pulling her closer...still closer.

A delightful groan escaped and the sound of her own voice caused her to open her eyes. At first glance, she didn't recognize her surroundings as sunlight poured in through the wide windows. Then, without any doubt, she realized she was in the barn, up in the hayloft, spooning with Jake Scott.

Fortunately, she was still dressed.

She immediately pulled away from his grasp, but he didn't wake. Instead, he merely rolled over and continued sleeping. For a split second, she wondered if he was pretending to sleep. She was about to nudge him, but then thought better of it.

She hadn't gotten up once during the night to hose down Sweet Girl, nor had she been able to apply the ointment. Certain that Sweet Girl was in horrible pain, Kenzie was about to run down to her stall when she spotted one of the tubes that Coco had left lying next to Jake. It was now almost empty. Jake had apparently done double duty.

"Thank you," she whispered, thinking how sweet of him to let her sleep. Maybe he did have a kind heart under all that bravado, after all. She slid a wisp of hair off his forehead, then gently covered him with the blankets, dusted herself off and made her way down the stairs.

When she checked on Sweet Girl she seemed fine, and from the looks of the wet ground in front of her stall, it appeared that she'd recently been hosed down and a fresh coat of ointment had been applied.

Jake had turned out to take better care of Sweet Girl than she did. She certainly couldn't hate him now. As she walked to the house, all she could think about was how safe and warm she felt snuggled up against him.

As if she belonged there.

As if they were lovers.

And as much as she didn't want to admit it, she had liked it, liked it more than she had ever imagined she would. It had been a long time since she'd felt that much warmth and caring from a man. Too long. And now that she had a taste of that kind of gentleness she didn't want it to stop.

"This is not good," she mumbled as she approached the back door to the family ranch house, feeling a slight headache behind her eyes.

But she didn't have time right now to be thinking of Jake's warmth, or how she felt with his arms wrapped around her, or how he looked when he was sleeping or the fact that he'd taken care of Sweet Girl while she slept.

Who does that?

She forced herself back to the reality of the ranch and what her objectives were for the day. She hoped it was still early enough for her to check on the livestock, especially the new calves. She wanted to personally make sure they were cleaned and had enough feed. She gazed up at the kitchen clock that had been hanging in the same spot next to the stove ever since she could remember. The clock she'd learned how to tell time on. The clock she'd watched when she'd waited for Santa to slide down the chimney. The clock that had ticked off the long seconds when she'd waited for her date for prom, and the clock that now told her it was almost nine thirty.

"Not again!"

It seemed impossible. She hadn't done this since high school, or maybe even elementary school. She had no idea what was causing such a shift in her personality, but she knew it had to stop.

Kenzie assured herself that she was done with fooling around, not to mention messing up…and she was most especially done with getting all sentimental over Jake. Sure it had been nice to spend the evening with him, to finally understand why he'd laughed when she kissed him and, heaven help her, to sleep next to him. But ever since he'd arrived she'd lost focus, and there was no time for that. Especially now that her inability to say no to him had caused Sweet Girl her injury. She needed to keep the ranch humming, and getting sidetracked by Jake Scott was not something she could afford to do, not if she wanted to maintain the place and its current upward swing.

"And whose idea was it to spend the night in the barn with me? His! He knew exactly what he was doing."

She knew if he hadn't been there, she would have set her own clock on her phone and taken care of Sweet Girl. Now she was beholden to him, and he probably had planned it like that all along.

She didn't believe that was 100 percent true, but she never would have slept so peacefully if he hadn't been there with his big strong body next to hers. It was just another example of his sly little tricks to weaken a woman's resolve.

Once Kenzie had showered, slipped on a lacy white bra and matching panties...not that she was planning on anyone seeing her undies...she chose some clean jeans and a cream-colored T, dried her hair, added a bit of makeup and tugged on her boots. She was out in the kitchen ready for her first cup of coffee in less time than it took for her to even think about waking up in his arms...over and over again.

No matter how she tried, she couldn't shake the warm feelings that were growing inside her for Jake.

She'd made a few calls to the shipping company, to no avail. She'd also called customs, but got nowhere. To say she was frustrated with the whole thing was an understatement.

She entered the kitchen, hoping to find a pot of Jake's coffee waiting for her. Instead, the pot sat empty in its stand. Disappointed, she grabbed the jar of instant, dumped a heaping spoon in her empty mug, ran the water in the sink until hot, slipped her mug under the faucet, then turned for the milk in the fridge.

She spotted the note stuck to the refrigerator door with specific instructions on how to make a pot of Jake's coffee.

Kenzie stared at the note, deciding. No one was around. She could make the coffee and clean out the pot so no one would be the wiser.

No way did she want anyone to know she actually liked Jake's coffee. It would be like admitting she liked Jake…which she was trying her best not to do.

She moved with the efficiency of someone who'd done this a million times, at least, that was what her delusional mind conjured up. However, by the time she took her first delicious sip and eyed the messy trail she'd left behind, she realized this coffee-making thing was going to take a bit of practice.

"Good, huh?" Her mom's voice startled her, causing her to spill coffee down the front of her shirt. Dora and Dolly padded over for some loving, which Kenzie gave them. Then they settled next to the back door in their usual spots on their oval braided rugs.

"Oh, honey, I'm so sorry," her mom consoled. "I didn't mean to scare you. Did you burn yourself?"

Kenzie placed her mug down on the counter then tugged at her T to view the damage. The coffee stain ran down the center. No burns, but she'd have to change her shirt.

"No. I'm fine."

"Are you sure, sweetheart? Because, well, I have to say that lately—"

Kenzie could tell her mom was fishing for more than wanting to know if she'd burned herself. Kenzie's mom had a way of getting to the truth of the matter with simply a minor inflection of her voice.

"None of the coffee soaked through, mom."

"I'm not just talking about the coffee, but I think you already know that. How's Sweet Girl?"

"She's fine. I, well, actually Jake, took good care of her last night while I slept."

"He's a good man. Caring. But how are you holding up?"

Her mom came over to her, and gently slipped a strand of Kenzie's hair behind an ear. From the time Kenzie was a little girl, she always thought her mom was the most beautiful woman in the world.

She still believed that.

Her mom, Mildred, had a deep, rich voice. Her long chestnut-colored hair, that now showed some gray streaks, had been clipped up in its usual bun at the nape of her neck. Mom was a thin, shapely woman and still wore a cowgirl hat when she worked outside, and a frilly apron when she cooked. She didn't like her hair flying in her face, had crystal blue eyes, thin skin with very few lines, and she always wore deep red lipstick and mascara. But the best part of Mom was her smile. It could carry sunshine into a cave.

"I'm fine, Mom. I'm sorry if I've worried you or Dad the last couple of days, but I'm back together again. This is the last time I'll be getting up late, I can assure you of that."

"Sweetheart, you've been getting up at dawn since you were a babe. Probably do you some good to sleep in every now and then."

"Yeah, well, that's okay for other people, but not for me."

Kenzie reached for a sponge to mop up the spilled coffee, but her mom beat her to it. Then her mom proceeded to clean up the coffee grounds that had escaped the grinder and the water that had pooled on the counter when Kenzie had added it to the coffee maker.

"I can do that, Mom."

"I've got it. Ya know, nobody's perfect, honey. Sometimes you have to allow other people to help you, to show you an easier way. There's no shame in that, sweetheart."

Kenzie decided to ignore her mom's advice. Normally, she welcomed it, but on this subject, Kenzie knew what she had to do, and it didn't include help from anyone.

"I'm all grown up now, Mom. I don't need you to be cleaning up after me."

She held out her hand for the sponge.

"Well, maybe I like to clean up after you, to help you, to be here when you need me. You haven't asked for my help or opinion in a long while. Maybe too long. I admire that you're determined to do everything on your own terms. You have a lot of me in you, and I expected it when you were a teen and even when you went off to college. I knew you'd want to stand on your own. But goshdarnit, ever since you took over this ranch you've locked up your feelings so tight I don't know who you are anymore. We hardly talk, and now that Coco has moved to town…well… unless I can get you to open up more, all my daughters will be on their own. Even you, and you're just down the hall."

Kenzie's eyes watered. She had no idea her mom had been feeling so left out. She'd been the family rock all of Kenzie's life, even stronger than her dad in some ways. Kenzie had strived to be like her.

Strong.

Independent.

A self-starter.

She could handle any situation that was thrown at her, except perhaps her babies growing up and living on their own.

Kenzie wrapped her arms around her mom. "I love you, Mom. You know that. You're my hero, and I've always wanted to be just like you. I know all the stories of how you ran this ranch all by yourself when you were only seventeen while Dad was in Vietnam. You single-handedly made the ranch profitable, and when Dad came home, he couldn't believe that his "city wife" had not only learned how to foal a horse, but could chop down a tree and split the logs to get her through the winter. You both waited until he came home to have a family because that was the responsible thing to do. I work as hard as I do because I know how much this place, our family legacy, means to you and Dad. I want to prove that I'm as responsible as you and dad were. I don't want our family to lose it on my watch."

"You don't have to prove anything to us, sweetheart. You mean more than this ranch ever could. You have to know that. All our kids do. We'd give it up in a heartbeat if it meant that you'd be happier doing something else, something that might be more fun. You need to have fun, child. Go out and laugh with your friends, with your sisters, with Jake. I haven't seen you take a day or night off in months."

"I took a night off just last night, Mom, and Sweet Girl got hurt and I overslept…again."

Kenzie sipped the coffee, wanting to moan with delight. She couldn't believe coffee could taste so good. She'd been drinking it for the caffeine rush, not the flavor. Even her mom's coffee didn't taste this good.

Her mom pulled out one of the wooden chairs around the kitchen table. "Don't be so hard on yourself. You deserved a night off. Now, pour your mom a cup of that great-tasting coffee and tell me all about your night off. Where did you go?"

"Just to Belly Up."

Kenzie poured coffee into her mom's mug, added milk and brought over the bowl of sugar. Then she calmly sat down across from her.

"Were you and Jake on a date?"

"Mom, you know how I feel about Jake."

"I thought I did, but now I'm not so sure. It seems like you resent him, and I can't understand why, exactly."

Kenzie drank down some of her delicious coffee.

"Mom, I don't resent him. I'm just not happy with the reason why he's here, and if you're wondering, nothing happened in the barn last night."

"That's none of my business, but you've always had a soft spot for that boy, the way you used to follow him around when you were little. I always thought you two were perfect for each other…full of spit and fire."

Kenzie stood up. "Is that what all of this is about? You and dad…matchmakers? Is that the real reason why he's here?"

"Don't be silly…but if it works out that way… well—"

Kenzie didn't like any of this. Was she falling for a guy her parents picked out for her? "I can't believe that you and Dad would do this. And apparently Carson was in on it, as well. Probably my sisters, too. Well, I don't like it. I don't like it one bit."

Kenzie stood, poured more coffee into her mug, then turned and rested against the counter.

"Yep. Spit and fire! Now give me your shirt and I'll soak it."

Her mom held out her hand. Kenzie wanted to storm out, but this was her mom. Nobody in this family stormed out on Mom.

She pulled off her shirt and handed it to her mother. Her mom left the room, with the dogs following close behind her while Kenzie added more milk to her cup then put it back in the refrigerator just as Jake Scott walked into the kitchen.

Her initial reaction was to hide and cover up. She didn't really want to deal with him first thing in the morning, especially after last night, and more especially because she was seminude. But given Jake's silly grin, she wasn't about to cover anything. Did the man have some sort of sixth sense or what?

She refused to blush, and instead ignored his presence.

"If that's what you're wearing today, you might reconsider," he said, grinning. "It's a bit chilly out there this morning."

JAKE WALKED OUT of the kitchen with a big smile on his face. It just kept getting more and more interesting as each day passed. Even if he'd wanted to stay away from Kenzie, fate seemed to be pushing them together with one situation after the next.

He'd gotten up early to hose down Sweet Girl, then couldn't go right back to sleep, so instead he'd worked with the cattle for a few hours using natural persuasion. He'd crashed again for a few hours in the loft next to Kenzie and as soon as he had, she'd snuggled right up next to him. It had taken all his restraint not to wake her with a kiss, but in truth he'd been dog tired after spending half the night tending to Sweet Girl, so he'd fallen asleep holding Kenzie close. A position he relished.

He'd cleaned up in the guesthouse and was about ready to the pasture the livestock, but first he'd wanted to check to see if it was all right with Kenzie. He thought he'd give her a demonstration first of how he'd used gentling to get her cattle to trust him. He'd had no idea she'd be standing in the kitchen in her sexy little bra.

"Don't you ever knock?" Kenzie said as she caught up to him.

"I didn't think I needed to. I mean, you know I'm staying here, and until we completely finish up on that guesthouse, I'm living inside the main house. But what do I know, maybe you always run around in your underwear."

"I spilled coffee on my shirt and my mom went off to soak it."

"I guess I just have good timing."

She'd slipped on a black T-shirt, but he couldn't repress the vision of her standing next to the counter in a white lacy sheer bra. Then there was the memory of her body up against his last night and this morning. That memory tormented him, especially now. He really did not need to see her in her underwear, too.

"I guess you do," she said, with a slight smile. "Look, about last night. Thank you for taking such good care of Sweet Girl, but you should have woken me up. You didn't need to do all of that by yourself."

He stopped walking and turned to look at her. "No

problem. Besides, you looked too cute curled up next to me. I didn't have the heart to wake you."

Her face flushed. "About that, I'm sorry if I, um, used you for a pillow."

"Believe me, it was my pleasure."

"And what's that supposed to mean?"

"Nothing. I just didn't mind, is all. You tucked in next to me like you belonged there, and I liked it. I think you did, too."

He caught the grin tugging at the corners of her sweet mouth. "I may have, but that doesn't mean anything. I was just tired and I didn't know what I was doing."

"Sure. Okay. That makes total sense, especially after that contented sigh I heard this morning right before you got up."

"You heard that?"

"Uh-huh."

"Then why did you pretend to still be asleep?"

"I wasn't pretending exactly, it was more that I was dead tired and when you jumped up, I knew you weren't in any mood to acknowledge that sigh. But it was real nice, and it wasn't the only one. There had been several. I could only imagine what those sighs meant."

"Well, get your mind out of the gutter. I was dreaming about riding Sweet Girl."

He nodded, but he could tell by her face that there was much more going on in that dream than just a journey on her horse.

He wanted to talk about the previous night, about

the fun they had at Belly Up reminiscing about their lives. He wanted to get to know her better, confess his apprehensions about getting involved with a woman after coming off his bitter divorce. He wanted to spill everything and be honest with her, but she cut him off.

"I don't suppose you and Carson were able to move my heifers to the new pasture this morning?"

He liked how she could change the subject so easily.

"Um, no, but they're ready for it now. I called Carson and told him my plans, but he had a few commitments at the riding school. I told him not to worry. You and I can move them, if that's what you still want to do."

She shook her head. "It's too late in the day. Their bellies are full. I won't be able to lure them with food."

He figured she still used old methods to move small groups of cattle, old methods that depended on either aggressive movement or luring the cattle with hay loaded on the back of a pickup. He hoped she'd be excited to hear about natural persuasion, but he cautioned his enthusiasm. He reminded himself who he was dealing with: Kenzie Grant.

Right then and there, he decided he needed a new approach, one more in tune with what he used when he worked with his animals.

He needed to incorporate the methods of "gentling" with Kenzie.

He backed up a bit and gave her some space. Then

he smiled and hooked a thumb into a belt loop, wanting her to feel comfortable around him.

At once he could see the change in her stance. Her shoulders went back, and the soft features of her beautiful face seemed to warm in the sunlight. He knew for certain he was on the right track.

"I've got another way to move them, if you're interested. I know you don't want me to tell you how to do things on your ranch, and I respect that. Believe me, I appreciate where you're coming from. I've known several small ranchers in Montana who had no choice but to sell their land to big corporations. I get it. But your mom liked what I showed her this morning, and suggested that I share it with you. Of course, you may feel differently about it. And that's okay. I'm just following up on your mom's suggestion."

Kenzie took a sip of coffee from her travel mug, as she seemed to be pondering his proposal. He wondered if she had her awful instant brew in that mug, or if she bothered to make his. The way he had it figured, if she'd made his, the chances of her saying yes right now, were pretty good.

On the other hand, if what she drank was her instant, no way would she agree to give him even one more minute of her time.

She swallowed and said, "Sure, show me what you've got."

"Darlin', you're going to love this!" He tried not to get too excited about the breakthrough, but he couldn't help himself. He took off like someone lit a match under him and headed for the round corral where he'd been working with her American Brahmans.

"And I'm not your darlin'," she yelled after him, but he couldn't help himself. At that moment, Kenzie was most certainly his darlin'.

THE RANCH SEEMED to be deserted except for her mares in the corrals, along with Jake's stallions that were now segregated in their own corral away from her mares.

Jake stood in the middle of a round fenced enclosure that was off on its own. The twenty-two American Brahman heifers that were supposed to have been moved at the crack of dawn now surrounded him. And even more surprising was the way they seemed to love Jake. She hadn't been able to get within three feet of any of them, ever. There were a little over a hundred American Brahmans all told on the ranch, but these were the only heifers. Eight calves had already been born, and eighteen more were due anytime in the next couple of weeks. She felt really proud of the herd she'd increased twofold in just a little under three years.

For the next half hour, Jake demonstrated "gentling" to Kenzie while he held on to his rope, holding it out now and then as a guide. She'd heard the term *gentling* before, but always thought it was more trouble than what it was worth. She'd even tried it a few times, with no success.

What she couldn't believe was how her heifers

seemed to love him, and nudged him to pet them, even the young bull.

What was he? Some sort of cow whisperer?

"Okay, you've got me interested," she told him as she stood on the outside of the metal corral. "How are you able to get so close to them? And now that you can, how are you ever going to get them to move where you want them to?"

"By making kissing sounds instead of harsh *tsk*-ing noises. Kissing sounds keeps them calm. Plus, I never raise my voice, and I show them respect. I also try to remain mellow and show them acceptance for what they want to do."

The heifers kept moving around the corral, but not once did they walk over to her side, which was usual for them. She had always used a harsher persuasion method that worked on their fears. It was what she knew.

"Okay, but how will you get them to move to the new pasture? They seem pretty content right here."

"Well, why don't you open that gate, and I'll show you."

Kenzie hesitated. If the heifers scattered, it could be difficult and dangerous getting them all contained once again. Of course, if they did scatter, then she'd win her argument against Jake's "gentling" philosophy without saying one more word about it.

She walked into the tack shed next to the corrals, replaced her mug with a rope, walked back out and unlatched the gate. She wasn't taking any chances.

"They're going to be afraid of you, so it might work best if you follow for a while."

She agreed, and in less time than it took for her to settle her rope in her hands, Jake had all twenty-two heifers and one agreeable bull out of the gate, herded together and following the sound of his kisses. Not only did they stay right with him, but he could slow them down and speed them up with simple movements. Not once on the half-mile walk did they run or stray from their tight little formation, with Jake walking right alongside of them for most of the trek. And not once did any of them lag behind. No doubt due to her continuous pressure from shoring up the rear.

She tried the kissing sounds in order to keep them going, and to her amazement, the heifers reacted much more positively.

When they were all safely secured behind the fence that surrounded the pasture, Kenzie had to admit she never would have believed it if she hadn't seen it for herself. Not only had the move gone smoother than any of her other pasture moves had gone, but the animals seemed eager to please Jake, as if they'd been trained for months.

"How long did it take you to get them to react to you like this?" she asked as they stood together watching the heifers meander to their own spots in the pasture. She loved watching her animals graze. Usually she was on horseback when she led them to the next pasture and didn't hang around much after they were secured. This had been an entirely different experience.

She remembered her dad and mom leading cattle around using a similar way when she was a kid, before they'd expanded their land holdings, before the ranch began to lose money and they had to sell off most of their cattle at a loss.

"I've been working with them on and off since early this morning. Maybe about five or six hours."

These heifers and the young bull had been in this pasture a few times before, but it had always been stressful getting them here. This had been as easy as walking a trained dog in a park.

"This is fine for a small group of heifers. They're young and pliable. What happens when you have an entire herd of several hundred and they've been around for awhile, cows that are four or five years old?"

"Same method, only on a grander scale. And obviously, I wouldn't do it alone, and I wouldn't do it without a horse under me. But I can get the same results. We use it all the time on my ranch."

She didn't fully believe what he was saying. It seemed impossible.

"I'd like to see that."

"Then drive back with me after your parents' anniversary, and I'll show you."

"I may take you up on that, Jake Scott."

"You don't believe it's possible, do you?"

"Honestly? No, I don't. I think once again you're not being completely honest. For one thing, the manpower, and the time it would take to train my animals, I can tell you right now, would be cost prohibitive. Three man-days for every group of twenty animals just so we can pet them seems ridiculous when I can use my methods and move them without all that overhead cost."

"It's a onetime cost, then you're done."

"Not exactly. It's a cost each year with each new animal. The numbers just don't add up. As peaceful as these heifers are, this ranch can't afford it."

These were the sorts of practices that nearly lost the ranch before, and she wasn't about to try them again. She knew she was right, despite the fact that she appreciated the ease of this move.

"That's your choice, but in training the livestock, it will also benefit the trainer. You'd be surprised how relaxing it is to work with natural persuasion."

Her stomach tightened.

"So now this is all about me?"

"I never said that, but if you want to take it personally, that's up to you."

"You're a real piece of work. You think I don't know what you're trying to do?"

She turned on her heel, and started back up the path, avoiding fresh cow dung as she walked.

"Why don't you tell me, so we're both clear on that subject," he said, walking alongside her now.

"You know perfectly well you're trying to prove your theory that women can't be cowboys, can't run a ranch as good as a man and can't do any of the cowboy things that men can do, like moving a herd."

Her hands instantly clenched tighter around her rope.

"Now, where the heck did you get that idea?"

"From you."

"That's impossible. I never said any of those things, nor do I believe them."

"Yes, you do. You told me time and again when we were kids and I intend to prove you wrong at Cowboy Days over at M&M Riding School this weekend. So dust off your spurs, cowboy, and get ready to hustle, 'cause I intend to out-cowboy you on every level."

"Okay," he said. "Let's settle this thing…whatever it is. I'm game to compete in Cowboy Days if you are. And if you don't win your events?"

"Oh, but I will."

"Let's make it interesting. If you don't prove that you're the better cowboy, you owe me a kiss." He walked in real close, close enough to touch her body with his. A flash of heat ran through her when he lowered his voice to almost a whisper. "And not a simple little grandma peck, but one of them alley cat kisses you told me about when I first arrived."

She narrowed her eyes, and stared up into his, refusing to back down.

"Fine, and if I win, then you can pack up your 'gentling' ways and your brawny stud horses and your coffee bean grinder and go on back home."

He spit in his right hand, and held it out to her. "Then you got yourself a bet, Ms. Kenzie Grant."

She spit into her hand and grabbed hold of his with a grip that could crush steel, refusing to show any form of weakness.

When they let go, she wiped her hand on her jeans and walked back toward the house, wondering why the heck she'd made such a high-handed bet with a man she not only had growing feelings for, but enjoyed being around more than she ever thought possible.

Chapter Six

Jake moved into the guesthouse the very next afternoon. He'd found the source of the stench, a dead possum, and once he removed it, the place really improved. They'd forgotten to open the windows before they left, so Joel went around and did just that. He fixed the warped floorboards under the window, while a cleaning crew dusted, swept and scoured the home until it sparkled. Jake made the beds with fresh linens, stacked all the dishes and flatware in the dishwasher, and that evening he finally got a full night's sleep in a bed he could stretch out on.

He hadn't said more than a few cordial words to Kenzie since they'd made their little wager, and from what her dad had told him, that was probably a good idea. According to Henry, the frozen semen shipment had finally made it out of customs, but seemed to be taking the slow route down to the ranch. Kenzie was barely holding it together. It didn't help that Henry had once again suggested Jake's stud horses as an alternative. That, according to Henry, only set her stress levels higher.

Jake contemplated all of this while he tried to wake up under the shower, the water a mild temperature of cold.

And just as he was about to rinse the soap out of his hair, he thought he heard Kenzie's voice echo through the sound of rushing water. He ignored it, and stuck his head under the water to rub out the soap.

And before he could get the water out of his ears, the shower curtain slid aside and Kenzie Grant stood staring at him, arms folded, foot tapping, looking like she could spit nails.

He grabbed a washcloth and held it in front of the important parts. "Don't you knock?"

"About as much as you do."

"But I'm taking a shower."

"I can see that," she said as her gaze quickly swung over his body.

"Whatever you're mad about this time can wait until I'm finished."

"No, it can't."

"Fine," he said. "Have it your way." And he moved the washcloth to scrub his body.

She immediately slid the shower curtain back to give him some privacy.

"Thank you," he told her over the rushing sound of the water. When he finished bathing and turned off the shower she handed him a white bath towel through the curtain opening. He toweled off, wrapped it around his waist, then stepped out of the tub.

"Now, what's so darn important that you had to break in here and tell me while I'm taking a shower?

Did somebody die? 'Cause if that's not the emergency, I can't imagine why you would be so rude."

He walked past her and into his bedroom to get dressed. He had no intention of standing around listening to her wrath half-naked.

She followed him inside.

"Do you mind?" he asked as he grabbed a clean pair of jeans out of his suitcase.

She hesitated, but then turned around. "Don't go acting so innocent. I know you unlatched both Morning Star and Sweet Girl's gate this morning. I knew you were a low-down scoundrel, but I never thought you were this low."

Jake slipped on briefs, then his jeans and zipped them up. "I have no idea what you're talking about."

He grabbed a shirt, walked past her, and headed for the kitchen. Once again she followed close behind.

"Don't even try to act innocent with me, Jake Scott. This has all the markings of something you would do with your 'gentling' ideas. Were you trying to gentle my mare and your stud into mating this morning? Without my blessing? Trying to prove some misguided natural order of things?"

He had no idea what she was talking about and decided to ignore her…for now. Instead of paying attention, he sliced five oranges, then squeezed out the fresh juice with the electric juicer he'd brought from home. He pulled down two glasses from a cupboard, poured in the juice and handed her a glass.

She took it.

"I think you should start at the beginning, because you lost me."

She took a sip of the juice. "This is really good."

"I know. Orange juice is best when it's fresh."

She downed the juice then slapped the empty glass down on the counter.

"Don't try to change the subject."

"So far, I don't know what the subject is."

He had a hunch about what had happened, but he wasn't ready to admit to anything just yet. He needed a full stomach to adequately argue with Kenzie. As it was, his head still swam from a much-needed deep sleep.

"Your horse."

"What about him?" A pang of fright ripped through him when he considered that perhaps there had been an accident, that maybe he should actually listen to what she had to say. "He's okay, right? Or did something happen to him?"

"Morning Star is fine, probably more than fine… I'm not completely sure. You released him from his stall this morning, along with my mare. If I hadn't walked in when I did, well, I'm assuming I was on time before…before they coupled."

He shrugged. "But isn't that the idea?"

"That may be your idea, but it's not mine, and the mares belong to me. How dare you open those stalls when you know perfectly well that my shipment of semen is on its way? And besides, Sweet Girl isn't ready to go out yet."

He pulled a pitcher of cream out of the fridge,

along with bacon, eggs, tomatoes, cheese and a ripe avocado.

"Can you back this up and start at 'Good Morning, Jake? How are you on this fine morning? Did you sleep well?'" He pulled out a frying pan from a cupboard under the counter. "How do you like your eggs?"

"What?"

"Eggs and bacon? They're both organic. I like scrambled. Would that be all right with you?"

She looked a bit confused, but in a good way. He was hoping the breakfast question would throw her off her game and calm her down a bit. She looked and sounded a little too harried this early in the morning. It wasn't good for either her health or his. Normally, he liked to take his time in the morning, listen to a little local news, maybe some good country music before he ran out to catch the day. Kenzie's intrusion had disrupted his morning pattern.

"Yes, that would be fine, but what about the open gates? Are you going to explain why you would do that?"

"I didn't, but you're not going to believe me when I tell you how it must have happened. So, instead, why don't you take a seat at the table? I'll make us breakfast, and unless my stallion and your mare are romping around on the open roads somewhere, maybe we can simply sit back and enjoy a nice meal together. I even picked up a loaf of fresh bread from Holy Rollers yesterday, and I have a couple raspberry scones in the freezer, just for you."

Her shoulders relaxed, and she leaned on one hip. Her face even brightened under that fancy cowgirl hat of hers.

"With coffee?"

He could tell his offer was taking hold.

"Absolutely," he told her as he pulled out a chair from the small table that stood in the middle of the tiny well-lit kitchen. If she sat down then he knew they could work this out; if she didn't, it was going to be a really rough day.

She sat down, took off her hat and gently placed it brim up on the table; chestnut hair framing the delicate features of her face cascaded down around her shoulders. She looked radiant this morning, despite her temper,

He took in the deep breath he'd been afraid to take since she first showed up in his bathroom.

"Now," he said as he slipped on the shirt he'd tossed over the back of the chair when he first walked into the kitchen. "What kind of latches do you have on the stall gates?"

"You know perfectly well they're spring-loaded slide latches."

"Those are a walk in the park for Morning Star. I'm surprised he didn't let all your mares out this morning."

He grabbed the baggie of ground coffee he'd previously prepared at the main house, measured out the appropriate amount, dumped it in the top of the coffeemaker, flipped the button and within seconds the room filled with the aroma of freshly brewed coffee.

He knew it would work like a balm on Kenzie who sat back in her chair.

She shook her head. "No way. That spring is tight. You're just trying to put the blame on your innocent horse." Kenzie countered.

"If you say so, but if you have a main latch, that's his favorite—it means he has that many more buddies to run with."

"So you're saying Morning Star is a serial escape artist?"

"Yep."

"And I'm supposed to believe that?"

"Despite what you may believe, I don't have any reason to lie to you." He grabbed two gray mugs from the stand, filled them with coffee and handed her one. She eagerly took it, poured in some cream from the pitcher on the table, took a sip and let out the smallest of moans. Her voice sent a shiver over his body.

"How gullible do you think I am?"

"You're not gullible at all. I'm just explaining that Morning Star is the Houdini of horses. Unless your latch has an actual lock on it, he'll eventually find a means to break out. It's in his DNA. His father was the same. Don't tell me you've never heard of this before?"

She stared into his eyes as she drank more of her coffee. He was telling her the truth, but he could tell she was skeptical. Morning Star could unlock almost any latch and had caused him a lot of grief for a long time until he found a latch that also screwed into the ground, and even with that one, Jake had found it close to being opened several times.

"If your coffee wasn't so darn good I'd have doubt. But yes, I've heard of it, and okay, I believe you. Anyone who can make coffee like this can't be all bad."

"Then we've come to a good point in our relationship. You believe me. So how about a second cup?"

She chuckled and his world brightened as she handed him her now empty mug. "Oh, we're just getting started."

"Is that a promise?"

"Absolutely."

KENZIE SPENT THE rest of the day cleaning out stalls, fixing any holes in the fence that surrounded her pastures, and making sure any calves that were born were clean, dry and vaccinated. Along with that, she had to make sure her ranch hands knew the day's chores, and the volunteers from the local high school groomed all the horses once they were brought in for the night. Then she checked all the slide latches on the stalls to make sure they were secure, and gave Morning Star a good talking-to, not that she believed Jake for one minute.

But still, she made sure his latch was secure before she went up to the house for Sunday dinner.

She hadn't been able to shake Jake Scott from her mind for the entire day, even though she'd made several attempts. She'd worked extra hard, and really focused on every detail of her day, but her mind always swung back to Jake standing naked under that shower. She even scolded herself for having some racy thoughts about the two of them sharing that shower, which only caused her to work harder.

By the time dinner rolled around, Kenzie was dead tired. She washed up and changed out of her work clothes and into an actual dress. Then she applied extra makeup and even wore a darker shade of lip gloss. By the time she walked out of her bedroom, the house was filled with the usual assortment of guests and family. Sunday dinners at the Grant house were more like events rather than just a meal. All three of her sisters were there, along with her two brothers-in-law: Kayla's husband, Jimmy, and Callie's husband, Joel. Joel's adorable young daughter, Emma, loved to play with Kayla's toddler, Jess. Even Father Beau had showed up, along with Carson and Zoe. Zoe was all about Mom and Dad's anniversary wedding next Saturday, and had brought over some swatches of fabric she wanted Mom to pick from for the top of the arbor Mom and Dad would stand under to say a few words to the guests. Zoe even brought her business partner, Piper, along so they could go over last-minute plans.

The house was jumping with people, but when Jake didn't show up, she grabbed a bottle of wine, put together a dinner care package that included a monster slice of her mom's apple pie, and walked on over to the guesthouse to make sure everything was all right. Dora and Dolly padded right along with her. She hadn't actually seen Jake since breakfast, and that experience still burned in her memory as she approached the brightly lit-up guesthouse.

Now she merely wanted to apologize for her rude behavior that morning. She figured that must have been the reason why he'd been invisible since then.

Her temper had once again gotten the best of her, and she regretted it. She'd been spittin' mad when she first went into the house. So mad that she didn't care if he was taking a shower. She was going to give him a piece of her mind, but seeing him naked only reminded her of the other night when she awoke cuddled in his arms. She could only imagine what it would be like to have sex with him, to make love to him, to be loved by him.

Not that she could ever admit it out loud, even to herself, but there was no doubt in her mind that kissing Jake Scott would clearly be a different experience than it had been the first time.

As she got closer to the guesthouse she spotted Jake out in front, roping the longhorns that normally hung over the fireplace in the living room. He had them secured to a garbage can while he whirled his lasso in a big circle overhead, then tossed it directly over the horns. Each time he succeeded he'd let out a *whoop.*

She couldn't help but chuckle at the sight. "Is this why I haven't seen you all day? Practicing your cowboy skills?"

He pulled in his rope, coiled it, then tossed it up on the porch. The two dogs ran over to him wanting some loving, which he gave freely.

"Just passing time. Nothing more."

But she knew better. Working a ranch was one

thing, competing in an event was something all together different.

Her skills were still pretty sharp from the previous Cowboy Days she'd competed in last month in Jackson, Wyoming, a town that was only a twenty-five-minute drive from Briggs. She'd entered for the experience and ended up winning All-Around Cowgirl. She liked to hone her abilities every chance she had.

"You missed dinner, so I brought you some, along with a bottle of wine. I figured you for a red wine drinker, considering all the health benefits in the stuff."

"Resveratrol. It's good for your memory and for your heart."

"You should drink the entire bottle."

He cocked his head to the side, and stared at her. "Why are you here, Kenzie?"

She didn't mean to be so sharp. "I actually stopped by to tell you I'm sorry for how I acted this morning. Not that I totally believe that Morning Star can work a latch, but I know enough about horses to realize that most of them are smarter than we give them credit for." She held up the wine. "Truce?"

A wide grin stretched across his lips. "Sure. I'll get some glasses and an opener. And thanks for thinking of me for dinner. I'm starved."

It was one of those perfect evenings—sunlight fading in the sky and kissing the clouds and causing them to blush a bright pink, a whisper of a breeze playing with her hair. Kenzie walked up the four steps and onto the front porch. She placed the bottle and the covered casserole dish down on the small side table in front of the bank of three windows, then made herself comfortable on the swing at the end of the porch, not far from the table. Her dad and brother had crafted the swing especially for the guesthouse, and Kenzie had always loved it. Apparently, so did Jake. Two throw pillows were piled in the corner.

Jake strolled back out onto the porch carrying two glasses, a bottle opener and napkins, and proceeded to uncork the wine.

"This is nice," he said, handing her a glass of the ruby red liquid. "Thanks."

"It's the least I could do."

He stood directly in front of her, just staring at her, holding his glass. "You look beautiful tonight, Kenzie. I don't think I've ever seen you in a dress before. It's lovely. And your hair, it's…well…you're beautiful."

"Thanks," she said, holding his gaze.

"Well," Jake said, then he took a sip of wine, and reached over slipping the lid off the casserole dish. "This smells great. Let me get a couple dishes and silverware."

He placed his glass down on the table and slipped inside. For a moment, she thought she should leave while she still had the strength, while she could still walk away, but he returned and with one look, she knew there was no turning back now.

He set the table and offered her a chair. She took it.

"Thanks," she said, putting her glass down on the table in front of her.

Jake took a seat, and they sat in silence while they filled their plates with sliced pork roast, gravy, mashed Idaho potatoes, fresh steamed broccoli lightly drizzled in lemon olive oil and homemade corn bread. Kenzie wondered what it would be like to be married to Jake, and to do this every night, right here on her ranch.

But then she remembered his ranch, his life…in Montana.

"I was sorry to hear about your divorce. That had to be tough," Kenzie said, attempting to break the tension in the air.

He ate a few bites of the pork and potatoes, but after another mouthful he put his fork down, took a sip of wine and began opening up. "I thought I'd found true love, and no one could tell me otherwise. I'm a bit of a blowhard, if you couldn't tell."

That relaxed her and she laughed. "Huh, I couldn't tell."

"Yeah, well, I don't mean to be… At least I don't mean to be now."

From the look in his eyes, Kenzie knew he was still hurting. "You must have loved her very much."

"That's just it. I think I loved the idea of being in love more than the reality of it."

He hit on a topic that she struggled with on a daily basis. "Kind of like actually running a ranch as opposed to dreaming about running one. I grew up glorifying the wonders of running my own ranch and couldn't imagine doing anything else from the time I was eight years old. Actually, I'm sure it was from the first time my family visited your ranch."

"And now? Now that you're completely in charge?"

Kenzie took another drink of her wine, it felt luscious and smooth in her mouth, and warmed her body on the way down. "I'm not so sure. I mean, I love ranching, and wouldn't want to live any other way, but I'm so scared all the time, stressed over every detail, every problem. I never thought it would be like this."

"Scared you're not handling it right? Scared you're doing too much? Too little? Scared your ranch is going to fall apart?" He smiled. "Sounds like my marriage. I couldn't seem to calm down. I wanted the marriage to be perfect and we were supposed to be the perfect couple. I think I married Heather because I thought she would make the perfect wife for me, and the perfect mother to our children. Shows you what I know about love."

Kenzie could absolutely relate to what he'd been going through. "I'm a little like that myself. Love for another person or for this ranch scares me."

"Why? What are you so scared of?"

And there it was, the question that Kenzie had been avoiding ever since she took over the ranch from her parents. She slipped off her chair and sat down on the swing, bringing her glass of wine with her. Then she gently pushed herself on the swing.

"That I'm not enough. That nothing I do or can ever do will be enough."

He came over and sat next to her on the swing.

Suddenly she wanted to take back her confession. Rewind her words. She never liked admitting weakness, and she especially didn't like admitting it to Jake Scott, despite his own revelations.

"That's just fear talking."

"Maybe so, but fear has no place with success. Determination is what it's all about and I have plenty of that."

"Always have. Spunk and fire, that's Kenzie Grant."

She drank down her wine and stood. "It's getting late and we have a big day tomorrow. Cowboy Days start bright and early. I better go."

He stood as well. "Kenzie, there's so much more I want to say, so much more we should talk about. Please don't leave. Not now. Not when we're finally being honest with each other."

"That's the problem. I can't——"

Then she leaned up and kissed him, without giving it another thought. Kissed him hard, and when their tongues touched, a fire ripped through her gaining heat as it spread out to her fingers and toes. He slipped his arms around her and pulled her in tight up against his strong body. She loved the way he felt pressing against her, all muscle and lust, loved the way he smelled, tasted.

And this time, he didn't laugh. This time a husky groan reverberated from deep inside him, and her knees went weak. His kiss was much more than she had ever imagined it to be. Passion and desire tore apart her reasoning, until she could barely think at all. Pure instinct wanted it to go on, wanted him to make love to her, needed him to touch her like she'd never been touched before. Every fiber in her body cried out for him.

"Let's go inside," he said. "Let me love you."

His words broke the spell she'd been falling under, and once again reminded her that this could never work. That nothing good could come of her falling for Jake Scott. She knew for certain now, that once she spent the night with him, there would be no turning back, and no way to work it out.

She slipped out from his embrace. "I can't... We can't. I have to go."

"No. Please. Stay."

He reached his hand out for hers, and she wanted to take it, but couldn't.

His eyes burned deep into hers, and it took every ounce of strength she had to move away from him, from his touch, his embrace. She knew this could only lead to heartache. It was a mistake to have kissed him, and it would be a monumental mistake to spend the night. They were each dedicated ranchers from two different states. She could never leave her ranch, and he could never leave his.

"This can't work," she told him. "You have to see that clearly now. This was a mistake."

Then she ran down the stairs, nearly tripping on the last step, with Dolly and Dora following close behind.

"I DON'T UNDERSTAND. Women compete alongside the guys?" Jake asked Carson as they drove up to the

M&M Riding School. Jake was the passenger inside one of the Grant ranch trucks, a truck that had seen better days. When Jake had asked him about all the dents in the truck, Carson told him that a misguided Brahman bull had had its way with it two years ago when the Grant family had hosted the event on their ranch. Since then, his dad had decided no more Cowboy Days for them.

"Remember, this isn't anything formal. It's more of a local event to kick off the summer. We used to break it out, different age groups, et cetera, but the adults didn't like that, so now we have two groups. Everyone under the age of fifteen is in one group, and everyone over sixteen competes in the adult activities. Heck, this year we even have real stagecoach rides and all the money collected goes to the scholarship fund for the riding school. Colt Granger and his brothers decided to invest in a real stagecoach. Travis Granger spent the last year restoring it, and let me just say, it's a beauty."

"I'll check it out. So, the title of All-Around Cowboy can go to either a guy or a girl?"

Carson nodded. "Yep. Wade Porter won it three years ago. He owns the ranch right next to ours. And Kenzie has won it the last two years."

"Sounds like it's going to get interesting out there."

Carson pulled the truck into a dirt parking space just on the other side of the metal archway for the M&M Riding School, killed the engine and turned to Jake. "So tell me, what the heck is going on with you and my sister that you entered this shindig? Why not just relax and enjoy the day instead of competing?"

Jake swung open his door. "I'm just trying to keep up with your sister, and so far, it hasn't been easy."

After Kenzie had left last night, Jake sat out on that porch for what seemed like hours hoping she would return and wondering if he should just go knock on her bedroom window. He'd gone up the path several times, but then always turned around again. Later, when he dropped into bed, he was so exhausted from fighting with himself that he instantly fell asleep and only woke up when the alarm on his phone went off in the morning. Never in his entire life had a woman kissed him like that, nor had he ever kissed a woman like that before, as if all his senses had been turned on for the very first time.

He'd expected Kenzie's kiss to be good, but never in a million years had he expected it to send his body and soul to another universe. Now he understood why he'd laughed when he'd kissed her when he was a teen. Now he remembered that kiss as clear as the day it happened.

He'd been embarrassed by the power of it, by the sheer force of that kiss. It was the only way he'd known at that young age how to react to that kind of emotion.

He'd laughed.

Well, he wasn't laughing now. Her kiss had thrown him completely off-kilter, and he had to find a way to tell her.

The two men stepped out of the truck, slammed

their doors shut and met around back of the vehicle. "Take it from somebody who knows firsthand, none of my sisters are easy, and Kenzie just might be the most strong-willed of the bunch." They walked toward a green three-story building, as Carson went on about Kenzie. "Not that I'm saying there's anything wrong with her independent ways. Our mom is like that: one tough woman. I'm proud to be her son, but Kenzie is in a league of her own. She started practicing roping and riding when she was barely out of diapers. She was only thirteen when she could rope a calf almost as fast as I could, and when she hit fifteen, she won her first mounted shooting competition. So, tell me how well you stack up on all these events, or it's going to be a bloodbath out there."

Jake's dad had taught him and his brothers to do most everything in a rodeo except barrel racing. "I'll be able to hold my own, and then some."

Carson stopped and looked him in the eye. "Good luck with that, 'cause the money's going on my sister."

Jake chuckled.

"Probably a wise bet. The more I'm around your sister, the more I'm realizing she's a force I'm ill-prepared for."

"Well, my man, dust off your spurs, because most of the women in these parts are a force to be reckoned with. They come from strong stock, that's for sure. There's a fire in their bellies that can't be put out."

Jake smiled and shook his head. "Amen to that."

As they walked closer to the covered arena, Jake was impressed by what he saw around him. Not only was there a crowd of people already enjoying the beautiful day, but the school was perched on a hillside with a view of the majestic Teton Mountain Range, the Snake River below and the booming town of Briggs itself.

"When we were kids, she'd beat me at everything except bronc riding. She's the one who taught me how to win. I owe my career to my dad's patience, and to Kenzie's competitive spirit."

Apprehension crept up Jake's spine. When he signed up for this competition, he had no idea his ongoing battle with Kenzie was about to go public.

"So what you're saying is, I have my work cut out for me."

"What I'm saying is *GET READY TO RUMBLE*!"

But all Jake could think of was that kiss and how his whole world had changed last night. Now all he had to do was prove to Kenzie he was worthy of her.

Oh, yeah. Not a problem.

Chapter Seven

Kenzie blamed the fact that she was barely winning her events at Cowboy Days on that kiss she'd shared with Jake the previous night. Because of that impulsive moment her dang equilibrium was off, her stability shaken and her confidence questionable.

She'd only beaten Jake in calf roping by a fraction of a second, and he'd beaten her in the barrel race by almost the same margin. When it came to bareback bronc riding he won by an entire half of a second. His winning time had put her overall win in real jeopardy. Plus, whenever either one of them burst out of a chute the crowd went wild. Kenzie didn't want to believe it, but the town seemed to be equally divided between the two of them, as if they all knew there was something deeper going on.

And knowing how fast gossip spread through Briggs, she felt certain they knew about the kiss she and Jake had shared last night. She didn't know exactly how they knew, but somehow they did and thought the whole competitive angle between them was funny.

That thought just made her more determined than ever to win.

Cowboy Mounted Shooting happened to be the last event of the day. Helen Granger, who was the co-owner of the M&M Riding School and wife to Colt Granger, had won the national championship on her horse Tater a few years back. Tater was one of the finest mounts that ever ran the course. Helen had generously offered up Tater to Kenzie in a kind gesture.

Kenzie had spotted Carson giving last-minute pointers to Jake right before the bareback bronc riding event, so it was fair that Helen would not only offer up her winning mount, but also give Kenzie a few of her winning secrets.

"Remember, when you go into the back turn, holster your first gun as quickly as possible and pull out your second, taking aim as you do. Don't worry about Tater, he knows the course inside and out," Helen told her. "Just make sure to lean with him at all times. He won't let you down."

Tater, a honey-colored Nokota, seemed excited and ready to get out there to win, which Kenzie had no doubt he would. If her timing wasn't good enough, it would be Kenzie's fault, and not the horse's. She'd been practicing with him for the last hour, each getting used to the other, just like Jake had been practicing with one of the other horses that had been trained in mounted shooting. It took months of practice to get a horse ready for the event, and Helen and her team were experts at all the nuances.

Helen Granger was the type of cowgirl Kenzie

wanted to be when she grew up. Not that Helen was that much older than Kenzie, maybe five years or so, but Helen, with her strawberry blond hair and no-nonsense attitude, single-handedly championed the riding school and had made it the success it was today. She had the reputation of being a shrewd businesswoman, and a champion marksman. Plus, as far as All-Around Cowgirl went, Helen had it going on in spades.

"That's always been my problem. I'm not aiming when I draw the second time. I hesitate. Not this time," Kenzie assured her while on horseback.

"You've got this," Helen said, then gave Tater a loving pat on his long neck and left Kenzie to her thoughts.

Kenzie popped in the sponge earplugs, pushing each one deep into her ears. She knew that more than half the arena was out there making side bets like they did every year. Last she heard, the money was on her. Just knowing this caused her stomach to tighten and her adrenalin to surge through her veins.

She knew Jake's side bets were following close behind hers, or maybe by now they were both in a dead heat.

Not that there weren't many more contenders who could possibly win it all, but Kenzie's times, and Jake's times were the best so far. So it all came down to this event, and unless one of them made a huge mistake, either she or Jake would triumph.

"Good luck, Kenzie," Jake's voice echoed behind her. She turned and spotted Jake and his chestnut-colored mount moving up next to her. Tater shuffled under her, but she steadied him.

"You, too," she told him, smiling, trying to keep it light.

"Kenzie, about last night. We should talk."

The rider before her had finished and was now heading toward her through the open gate.

"And we will. Just not right now."

"No matter what happens in this competition, I'll do whatever you want me to do. Go or stay. It's up to you."

She didn't know what she wanted, especially not now when she was gearing up for the next event. She wanted to win, sure, but she also didn't want him to throw the competition.

"You can't give up now, Jake Scott. It's not fair. I expect you to give it your best."

He sat up straighter, a smile curved his lips. "I never said I was giving up on the competition. That's a given. I *never* give up on anything I want." He pulled his hat lower on his head. "Be prepared for the ride of your life! Jake Scott is in the arena, and he plays to win!"

Then he guided his horse back in line.

Now that she was completely thrown off-kilter, she quickly checked her two single-shot Cimarron .45s making sure they were securely set in their holsters on the belt that rested on her hips. The guns didn't shoot bullets, but rather black powder specially designed for the event. She pulled her cowgirl hat lower on her forehead, nodded to the previous rider as he passed her and eased Tater out into the arena.

Kenzie knew her family would be cheering for her along with several other townsfolk. So when she looked around and saw so many people up on their feet, yelling and applauding it gave her exactly the inspiration she needed to try for the best time.

But that kiss came rushing back, and the last thing she wanted was to see Jake leave. Oh, she was so confused, which wasn't helping her mental fortitude to win this thing.

She took a deep breath and let it out again, telling herself to concentrate, that this would be her fastest run ever. She tossed all her apprehensions aside and focused on the task at hand.

There was nothing that compared to the rush Kenzie felt each and every time she and a horse were about to compete. The sounds of the fans, the feel of the reins in her hands, the movement of a strong animal propelling her forward and the earthy scent of the rich dirt that covered the floor of the arena.

Tater moved in a fast canter as she guided him in a tight circle waiting for the buzzer, the anticipation pounding in her chest, directing her focus on that first red balloon.

The buzzer.

The roar of the crowd in the stands.

The rhythmic pounding of Tater's hooves as they connected with the ground.

Without thinking, the weapon was in her hand as she took aim at the first balloon. She hit it before

she could even register the sound…then the next…
and the next, until she was headed for the red barrel.

She quickly holstered her first weapon and pulled
the second .45 free, clicked the hammer back, and
aimed at the first white balloon while she guided
Tater around the barrel. She managed to pop each
of the five balloons on the run down and holstered
her firearm before she and Tater made it to the end
of the course.

Kenzie knew she'd have a winning time. Knew
she'd beat out the other competitors, but what she
didn't know, would it be enough to beat Jake?

"FOR THE FIRST time in our local Cowboy Days his-
tory," Mayor Sally Hickman, a stylish fortysome-
thing, middle-aged woman announced over the
loudspeaker inside the arena, "we have a tie for All-
Around Cowboy." The arena exploded in cheers and
whistles as everyone stood in the surrounding metal
stands. "The winners are Kenzie Grant and Jake
Scott. Let's give them a big Briggs congratulations!"

That scene continuously looped inside Jake's head
as he sat on a barstool inside Belly Up surrounded
by some of the townsfolk, including a woman named
Lana Thomson who kept coming on to him, her ruby-
red lips continuously puckered as if she was waiting
to be kissed. Not that he minded being around her,
she was a good-looking woman, but there was only
one beautiful woman he had his sights set on, and she
stood at the opposite end of the bar.

He still had a hard time believing that he and Kenzie had tied. There'd been other winners in different categories, but the All-Around was the most anticipated prize, and it had been a full-on tie, down to the same fraction of a second.

"It's unheard of," Joel told him as he stood next to Jake, holding a longneck beer in his right hand, his left hand on Jake's shoulder.

"Can't say that I've seen it but one other time down in Houston, about four years ago in bull riding," Carson told everyone. He sat on the stool on Jake's right.

"You looked like the wind during that last event. And your roping was pure perfection," Wade Porter announced more to the crowd rather than just to Jake. Wade seemed like a friendly enough cowboy, in his early thirties, with a knack for building stuff, at least that was the impression Jake had.

"When I was a younger man, I used to be able to ride and rope like that…or at least I thought I could," Hank Marsh said. "But watching you today, I realized, I was never that good. You were somethin'."

Jake had briefly met Hank Marsh at From The Ground Up during Kenzie's run through the store. They hadn't been properly introduced until tonight, when Carson called him over to meet Jake. Hank had a crop of white hair, a round belly and looked to be in his late sixties. But most of all, Hank had one of those welcoming smiles that made Jake feel right at home.

"You were a thing of beauty," Lana said in a wispy voice, while she rubbed his shoulder as if she knew him intimately.

"Have another beer on me," Milo Gump said from

behind the bar. Jake had the pleasure of meeting Milo, the owner of Belly Up, when he and Joel had first walked into the tavern earlier that night. He was a big round guy who wore a cattleman's hat the likes of which dated back to Hoss Cartwright on *Bonanza*.

"No thanks," Jake told him. "I've had enough."

"One more can't hurt," Lana said, then grabbed the beer and took a long drink. Jake and Carson shared a look, then smirked knowing that this woman was nothing but 100 percent pure trouble.

The many residents of Briggs had shown their love and support with well wishes, high fives and a multitude of handshakes. Jake was awestruck.

When he looked down the long bar, Kenzie had the same thing going on. Residents wishing her well, and congratulating her. More people flocked around her, and the laughter echoed throughout the tavern. Every now and then he'd catch her staring over at him, and he'd throw her a smile. Occasionally, she'd catch it and toss a smile back, but ever since Lana appeared on the scene, Kenzie had stopped the smile game.

Now that they both had tied for the All-Around title, and Kenzie had already held up her end of the bet with one mind-blowing kiss from the previous night, it was his turn to hold up his end of the bargain, and leave.

But he didn't want to leave, even more so now.

Still, he didn't really have a choice. He had to suck up some grit, walk on over there and offer to hold up his end of the bet, hoping like heck she would ask him to stay. He had to at least make the attempt. He'd already told her that he'd do whatever she wanted him to do...which had to be one of the more stupid things he'd ever done in his entire life.

Still, it was the right thing to do.

And he was going to march up to Ms. Kenzie Grant and do that right thing just as soon as he finished his beer.

"I'm going over there," he told Carson, once he took a couple more big gulps. Lana had set her attentions on Wade Porter, thank you very much. No one else could hear him. The other folks were busy recounting the day's events.

"Where?" Carson asked.

"To talk to your sister, Kenzie. We made a bet over who would win, and now that it's a draw, well, we need to clarify the results."

"What was the bet?" Carson asked, turning toward Jake who detected a slight smirk spreading over Carson's face.

"I'd load up my horses and leave if she won."

Carson eyes went a little wider.

"And if you won?"

"She owed me a kiss, but we—" Jake stopped talking when Carson held up a hand.

"You don't have to tell me more. I can see by the tortured look on your face that the kiss already happened. So now you think you should tell her you're leaving to hold up your part of the bet."

"Something like that, yes."

"Oh, man, I don't know. My dad said you've already caused her to rethink the fire retardant on the hay, and he saw her out there trying a different method on moving the cattle. He's really happy about the changes so far, and won't be happy about your leaving. Plus, their anniversary is only a few days away. I'm certain both my mom and dad would be disappointed if you left now. Mom already told me how much she loved your input on the dinner menu, and Joel mentioned that he needs some help with something he's trying to build. I'd think twice about how to honor that bet if I were you."

Jake had to do what was right or he couldn't live with himself, and seeing how hard Kenzie worked to win today, and watching her now laughing and talking with her sisters and their friends, he knew if he had even a slight chance with her, he'd have to man up to his bet responsibilities.

He slammed the now empty bottle down on the bar, muffled a couple belches and said, "I'm goin' over there. If I don't return in ten minutes, send in reinforcements."

No matter how Kenzie tried to accept sharing the win with Jake, she somehow couldn't do it. Or perhaps she simply didn't want to do it. Because of the tie, he'd be staying and the more he hung around the more she knew she wouldn't be able to rein in her feelings for him.

Not since that kiss.

What she didn't understand about last night was how everything could change so completely with something as simple as a kiss. How she could go from mildly liking him—despite his ornery, more natural ways of ranching, and for that matter, his natural way of doing almost everything—to out-and-out wishing he would stay. And not only stay, but move right into her bedroom. She knew he felt the same way, knew there was more to that kiss than merely their lips touching. Kenzie had felt a connection, a deep connection that would only be intensified if they ever made love.

Kenzie longed for his touch, for his caress, for his lips on hers.

Problem was, she'd been wrestling with those intoxicating thoughts for over twenty-four hours now, and all it did was cause her a lot of grief. And probably caused her the clean win. Truth was, though, that if she'd actually won, he'd be leaving and she'd be begging him to stay.

"Is now a good time?" Jake asked, startling Kenzie so much she let out a little "ooh!"

If she didn't know better, she'd bet he knew what she'd been thinking. She felt her face flush.

"Are you okay?" he asked, staring at her as if there was something wrong, which there most certainly was not. She cleared her tight throat, and pulled her blue shirt away from her body. Her clothes even felt restrictive, like she couldn't breathe if she didn't remove them soon. She could feel the heat building around the top of her shirt, down her legs, up her arms. Almost as if a hot rush of air had engulfed her.

"Sure. Couldn't be better," she told him, grabbing her cool beer, and taking a long swig, then pressing the bottle to her forehead. "It's just so hot in here. Don't they know it's time to turn on the air-conditioning?"

Jake looked up, pointing at the vent with the ribbon attached moving around from the breeze. "It's already on."

"Yeah, well, it's not enough."

A teaser of a smile creased Jake's lips as he stared at her. Okay, so she'd just made a fool out of herself over air-conditioning, but what else was new? She'd been running this routine for days now. Lately, it seemed everything she did or said around him hadn't come out right.

She just needed him to leave.

Or commit to stay…forever.

She cleared her clogged throat. "A good time for what?"

"For us to talk," he said, his eyes burning into hers.

"About today?" she asked, knowing perfectly well that wasn't what he wanted to talk about.

"Not exactly, but if that's what you want to focus on, okay. I told you I would do whatever you want me to do, and last I heard, you wanted me to leave, so I'll be heading out in the morning. That is if you still want me to go."

He'd caught her completely off guard. For a moment she didn't understand what he was saying. "But that kiss had—"

She was about to tell him that the kiss they shared had nothing to do with their bet. That kiss was…

well…she didn't know what it was exactly other than something she'd like to repeat…again and again.

"Yes, you held up your end of the bet with that kiss," he said, showing no emotion. "And now it's my turn to hold up my end. I can be ready to roll out around eight or so."

And there it was, Jake Scott at his finest. Once again she'd been stressing over their kiss, been worrying they'd had a connection, when obviously he'd never felt anything, or he wouldn't be standing there telling her he'd be leaving in the morning, rather than begging her to let him stay.

"Is that what you want to do?" she asked, staring into those emerald eyes of his, wishing he'd tell her that he couldn't go, not now, not ever.

"Isn't that what we agreed on?"

"Yes, but I—"

"Then I should head out."

She did a mental sigh, realizing his leaving was for the best, their best. Jake Scott belonged in Montana, on his family ranch, and she belonged here, in Briggs, Idaho, running her family ranch. The two of them had obligations. Their parents depended on each of them to do the right thing. Their siblings depended on them. Heck, looking around at everyone who'd made side bets, and all the well wishers and all the free beers lined up on the bar, maybe even the townsfolk depended on them.

"If that's what you think is best," she said, her stomach in a knot, and her throat thick with emotion.

It took everything she had to hold back the tears that threatened to betray her.

Their eyes locked and she thought she saw a glimmer of sorrow, a moment of indecision, but he blinked a couple times and it was gone.

"It's what we shook on, and I'm a man of my word."

Damn your word, she thought, but she couldn't bring herself to say it out loud, especially not in this environment, with half the town undoubtedly already speculating on a budding relationship between them. She didn't want to seem like the fool here, like the desperate woman wanting the big strong cowboy to stay.

She nodded, not wanting anything to slip out that might give away her secret. She didn't want him or anyone else to hear the lump in her throat when she spoke, or the feelings that would pour out. Instead she stood strong, like she always did when things got tough.

Her mother had taught her to face strife head-on, so that was exactly what she did.

"Then I'll see you in the morning before I go?" he asked, looking stoic. Looking like a man of conviction.

"Sure," she whispered, a forced smile pulling at the corners of her lips.

Then he turned and walked right past Carson, Joel and everyone else standing near the bar, even past Lana Thomson, who gave him a big sexy grin, and he headed right out of the glass front door and out of her life.

BRIGHT AND EARLY the next morning, before Kenzie had a chance to check to see if Jake had made good on his promise to leave, Coco pulled her SUV up to the back of the horse barn. She turned off the ignition, got out and made her way up to Kenzie as she and Chad, Kenzie's now-favorite high school volunteer, were unloading bales of untreated hay into the feed loft inside the barn from the bed of Kenzie's pickup. Kenzie had already given Sweet Girl some exercise earlier, so for the rest of the day, she would remain in her stall. Her wound was healing nicely, but Kenzie wasn't ready to let her out yet.

The hired hands had already moved her mares out to the corrals for the day, and Kenzie had no idea if Jake's stallions had been among them, or if he'd loaded them up and was already headed for Montana.

Several times during the night, she'd wanted to call him and ask him to stay and once she even put on a robe and slipped on her boots to walk over to the guesthouse to beg him to stay. Halfway there, she came to her senses and turned around.

Needless to say, she'd had yet another night without much sleep and couldn't adequately do her work because of it. The good thing was she'd gotten out of the house by five, the bad news was she felt completely exhausted, and even Jake's coffee wasn't helping this morning.

Because of it, Chad was doing all the heavy lifting. He carried another forty-pound block of hay into the feed loft without her help, along with about a week's worth of grain. The loft never held more than a two-

or three-day supply of hay. She always worried about a hay fire, and was even more worried now that this hay wasn't treated with a fire retardant.

After Jake's suggestion that her horses would be healthier eating untreated hay, Kenzie decided to give it a try, but she would keep the bales monitored for heat buildup. The rest of the load would be stored in another outbuilding on pallets where she or Chad or the ranch hands could easily check on its safety.

Punky peeked out of the passenger window. Kenzie knew that her sister kept a fuzzy red pillow on the seat to give Punky a few extra inches when he stood on his hind legs in order to see out. His little chin rested on the open window frame, golden eyes fixated on Coco. He was ready to pounce at any predator who might accost his mama.

"I'm sorry to have to tell you this," Coco began, using her official doctor's voice as she approached. "But your semen has been compromised."

"I don't know what that means, but it sounds really bad." Kenzie's stomach roiled, as she scratched her chin with the back of her gloved hand. She couldn't afford any more delays in that shipment.

"The breeder you chose to do business with used dry ice for shipping and because of the delays the dry ice evaporated, causing the semen straws to thaw. When they did eventually arrive at my office, they were completely worthless."

Kenzie sat down hard on one of the blocks of hay. "I can't believe this. Are you sure? Aren't there a few we can use?"

Coco threw her a look. "I'm sure. I checked."

Kenzie stood and pulled off her gloves, stuffed them in her pocket and began pacing in front of the open barn doorway. "Now I'll have to wait until next month. This throws off all of my plans for next year. I can *not* believe this."

Chad kept working, ignoring their conversation, hauling hay from the back of Kenzie's pickup. He was all of sixteen, already almost six feet tall, and one of the most competent volunteers she'd ever hired. He was going to make a superb rancher one day.

"You know, you really don't have to wait until next month," Coco advised. "You've got two stallions who I'm sure are willing to accommodate."

Kenzie was desperate enough to consider it now. Unfortunately, Jake had other plans.

"Even if I agreed to it, Jake has either already left or is in the process of leaving."

A wind blew up and Coco held on to her tattered ball cap. She wore a white Rascal Flatts T-shirt from the last concert she'd gone to, frayed jeans, not by design but from wear, and her normal laced boots. Her face was already taking on a slight tan from being out in the sun so much. Everyone in the family lathered on sunscreen these days, but Coco couldn't seem to remember it most of the time, thus the tan.

"Only because he's honoring a bet that you shouldn't be holding him to. It was a tie. You both won."

Kenzie had told her sister about the bet last night after Jake walked out of the tavern.

"He wants to leave," Kenzie told her, secretly wishing that wasn't the case.

"If I remember correctly, he didn't look like he wanted to go anywhere, much less back to Montana. And besides, Carson told me Jake was only leaving because you already held up your part of the bet. He told Carson he didn't really want to go, but felt he had no choice in the matter. Carson also told me that you and Jake kissed. Why didn't you tell me? What else happened? Did you sleep with him?"

Just then Chad walked out, trying his best to act like he hadn't heard what Coco had said, but Kenzie could see the gleam in his eyes.

"No, I did not sleep with Jake Scott." She turned toward Chad. "And don't you go spreading any gossip that I did. Now go on with your work and stop eavesdropping."

"Yes, ma'am," Chad said as he padded off, shaking his head, his cowboy hat nearly blowing off in the wind before he caught it and pushed it deeper on his forehead.

Kenzie hated when Carson went behind her back to one of her siblings with information that pertained to her.

"Why didn't Carson tell me that Jake didn't want to leave? That would've changed everything."

Kenzie folded her arms across her chest, hurt now that her brother and sister had been discussing all this between themselves. Plus, if she'd known about this, she might have been able to sleep last night.

Or not...

But at least she would have known the truth.

"You were too busy dancing on the tables."

Kenzie flashed back to the tavern. She didn't remember anything of the kind.

"I did no such thing. I would never lose control like that."

And as soon as Kenzie said it, she wanted to suck that statement back inside. Not only did she give Coco ammunition, but the words had hit a nerve deep inside Kenzie.

"That's for sure," Coco mumbled, her gaze gliding back to Punky. He moved around on the front seat, tiny nails clicking against the window frame, excited that Coco had noticed him.

"What's that supposed to mean?" Kenzie stuck a fist to her cocked hip.

"It means that you can't control everything. Just like the sperm. Sometimes you have to let go and let it be. See what happens."

"And let nature take its course?"

A flash of annoyance erupted inside Kenzie and she didn't like it. Kenzie and her sisters rarely, if ever, argued. They respected each other too much for antagonism. Even growing up, their mom had taught them to talk out whatever was bothering them without anger. Funny how Kenzie could pretty much maintain her cool with her siblings, but when it came to Jake Scott that had never been the case. Their relationship had always been a hot bucket of coal.

"Exactly like that, yes."

Kenzie let out the breath she'd been holding. "I

only want what's best for this ranch, for the livestock, and for Mom and Dad."

"True. We can all see how hard you're working to keep the ranch profitable, but sometimes you need to lighten up and take the olive branch when it's offered. It might work out better than you think."

"Or not."

"Well, it can't be any worse than dead semen, which is what you have now. Those mares have less than forty-eight hours before their time has passed. Ultimately it's your decision." Coco's face softened. "But you better make it soon, Kenzie, because Jake had pulled his rig up in front of the guesthouse when I drove over here to tell you."

Kenzie didn't want to admit her feelings for Jake, at least not straight out.

"There's more to this than just my letting go."

"You can deny it all you want, but I saw that disappointed look on your face last night when Jake told you he was leaving. I see it now. And from the dark circles under your eyes, I'd bet my entire house that you didn't get one lick of sleep last night fretting over him."

Kenzie wanted to argue, but out of all of her sisters, she never could hide anything from Coco.

"Maybe so, but there's no way anything can come of it. He and I have commitments that neither one of us can ignore. It's no good. It could never work out, so there's no use thinking that it can. He has his ranch and I have mine."

"Right now, I'm talking about your mares. All the

other stuff, the two of you can work out later. Seems silly for him to leave like this, when you obviously need his semen"

Chad walked out again. This time his eyes were about as wide as quarters.

"From his stallions, his semen from his stallions."

Chad kept his gaze on the ground, but the smirk on his face said it all.

"Fine," Kenzie said to Coco, hoping he hadn't already left. "I'll ask him to stay for the sake of the ranch."

"Great! Now all we have to hope for is your mares aren't as stubborn as you are, or we'll never get any foals," Coco teased.

Kenzie jumped into Coco's SUV and they high-tailed it over to the guesthouse.

She just hoped he wouldn't gloat.

Chapter Eight

Jake was just finishing up a bowl of Lucky Charms while sitting on the sofa in the guesthouse, when there was a knock on the front door. He figured it was Kenzie, eager to help him load his horse trailer that he'd driven out front about an hour ago. He still hadn't loaded his horses, nor had he gotten anything ready inside the trailer to secure his stallions.

Normally by this time in the morning he'd have been long gone, but for some reason he was dragging his feet. He hadn't even packed his suitcase, nor had he completely cleared out the bathroom or the kitchen. He'd been in the process of cleaning out the cupboards when he came across an unopened box of Lucky Charms, his childhood all-time favorite cereal. It didn't seem polite for him not to open up the box and have a bowl. He figured whoever put it up in his cupboard must have known it was his favorite, and he didn't want to seem like he didn't appreciate the gesture.

Knock. Knock. Knock.

"Be right there!" he yelled, right after he quickly

took the last big bite, then drank the milk from the bottom of the bowl. He jumped up and placed everything in the sink.

Jake had forgotten how good Lucky Charms were, or maybe it was because he hadn't eaten anything so laden with sugar in more years than he could remember. Either way, he'd be taking that box back home with him.

It was the polite thing to do.

He arrived at the door, put his hand on the knob, and readied himself for whatever Kenzie might throw at him, somewhat surprised that she actually knocked this time.

When he swung the door open, Joel Darwood stood on his porch looking like any typical cowboy: worn jeans, dark T-shirt, boots, the classic brown hat and a friendly grin. Just the sight of him threw Jake off center.

"Mornin'," Joel said, in a chipper voice. The guy always seemed to be in good spirits, probably due to the fact that he'd only recently married the lovely Callie Grant.

"Mornin'," Jake answered, trying his best to duplicate Joel's enthusiasm, all the while wondering about the nature of this early morning visit.

"Sorry to bother you, but I was hoping I'd catch you before you headed on out. Got me a real problem over at my place and I need some help. It won't take more than a couple hours of your time, and it would mean a lot to me, and to Callie."

Whatever Joel needed help with, Jake was ready

and willing to give. After all, Jake had driven out for that precise reason, to lend a hand on the Grant ranch, and considering Joel was part of the Grant family, and he and Callie were expecting their first baby, anything Jake could do to help out was fine by him.

"Not a problem. Be glad to in fact."

"I don't mean to keep you from your plans. I see you already moved your rig to load up. Are you sure?"

"Positive," Jake told him. "My plans can wait."

Jake didn't want to admit it out loud, but he didn't want to leave, at least not yet. Despite the desire he'd had when he first arrived to swear off women for awhile, he didn't want to go without exploring his growing feelings for Kenzie. Any excuse to keep him there for a few more hours was good enough for him.

"It's the arbor that Mildred and Henry will walk through once they arrive back at my ranch, after the church ceremony. I wanted to build something that would last, that I could give to the Grants for their own front yard once their anniversary was over and well, the arbor I ordered is too big and too heavy for me to finish it on my own. Do you think you—"

"Of course. Anything you need."

Jake grabbed his hat off the coat rack next to the door, and was out of the house before Joel could say another word.

"If you're sure?"

"I haven't been more sure of a decision in my life."

"Great. That's great, but I doubt it will take us more than a few hours. It's a surprise for Callie's parents. Zoe, she's the wedding planner, has a rickety little arbor we could rent, but I knew Callie didn't like it much. I decided to build one, on my own, which always seems to cause me problems. I mean, I've learned a lot since I've taken over the Double S Ranch, and everything was going good until I messed up the top of this thing. I took it apart a couple days ago, and now I can't seem to be able to put it back together again. I'm hoping you can help."

"The Humpty Dumpty factor," Jake said, chuckling.

"Exactly," Joel agreed, grinning.

Jake shut the door to the guesthouse and followed Joel out to his ranch pickup just as Coco and Kenzie pulled up.

Kenzie got out holding Coco's little dog, Punky, tucked in her left arm. His head twisted from side to side, trying to take in his surroundings.

"I thought you were leaving?" Kenzie asked as she approached. He wished he could read her, but so far, that ability had somewhat eluded him. Was she happy he was still there, or upset? He had no idea.

"I asked Jake to help me build something for the wedding," Joel answered, obviously trying to defend the fact that Jake hadn't driven off yet. "It should only take a few hours. I can't do it alone. It's a surprise for your parents."

Jake hung back to let the two of them work it out. He knew he was on borrowed time.

"What is it?"

"I don't want to say. I know how you and your sisters can't seem to keep secrets from your mom. I'm holding this one close."

Jake appreciated the interaction between Kenzie and Joel. Even though the guy had only been part of the family for less than a year, he seemed to know the dynamics. Loyal and true, not to mention salt of the earth. These were folks a person could believe in and rely on. Jake hoped he could fit in as well.

"Okay. I won't bug you."

"Thanks," Joel said and walked over to say hello to Coco, who remained behind the wheel of a bright red SUV.

Once Joel was out of earshot, Kenzie said, "You realize that one of Joel's projects could take a couple days instead of a couple hours. He has a habit of underestimating his tasks."

That sounded perfect to Jake. The wedding was less than four days away, and if he could somehow hang around until then, he felt certain that he'd get some alone time with Kenzie.

"Good to know, but however long it takes, I'll be helping him with it."

"I thought you were determined to leave?"

A warm breeze swept over the land and kept pushing long strands of Kenzie's hair into her face. Several times he'd wanted to reach out to move them, and several times he stopped himself. Maybe he should leave. It was getting more and more difficult for him to keep his distance.

"It'll have to wait until Joel and I finish whatever we have to get done, if that's okay with you. But I don't want you to think I'm trying to renege on my end of the bet."

Her demeanor seemed to soften. At least he was on the right track with his apology. "Then you don't mind staying?"

"I was leaving because you seem to want me gone."

"I thought you were leaving because of the bet."

She put him on the spot, but he'd always been good at deflecting a hit. He decided to push this back on her, on what he saw and felt from her the other night out on the front porch.

"I was, but in the light of day, I've decided I shouldn't be in a hurry. At least that's the impression I got the other night when we kissed."

Her face instantly flushed, as if a ball of heat had surrounded her. She glanced off toward the mountains, tucked a strand of hair behind her ear, then turned back to face him. The flush fading.

"You have no idea what my thoughts were during that kiss," she told him. Her voice low and husky reminding him of his first day when she told him she made love like an alley cat. He at once knew he'd hit a nerve, knew he'd said something that triggered a combustible reaction.

"Oh?" He loved to tease her. Always had since they were kids, but now it meant so much more. Now it meant he could get a glimpse into what she might be thinking, and that excited him. She'd always seemed to be in control and distant, but slowly he was making inroads into her thoughts, and he liked it, liked it a lot.

"What's that supposed to mean?"

"I was on the receiving end of that kiss the other night, and if I'm not mistaken, desire was about to consume us both."

She gazed down at the ground. "Well, you're very much mistaken. That kiss meant nothing."

He knew she was lying, knew she was trying to hold on to that double-checked facade of hers.

But he'd made a few dents in the armor and he intended to keep up the pressure.

"Can you look me in the eye and say that?"

She turned back to face him, whiskey-colored eyes burning into his as she quickly plucked something off his collar, then opened her hand. "Can you look me in the eye and tell me you didn't just eat a bowl of your favorite sugary cereal?"

He gazed at her open palm and there, glistening in the sunlight, lay a tiny blue marshmallow half-moon.

"You put that box of cereal in my cupboard to tempt me?"

"I sure did, and it proves you're not as 'natural' as you claim."

"And that kiss proved you're not as in control as you claim."

"Fine, so now what? You know this can't work between us. You know we both have commitments. It was just a kiss. Nothing more."

He moved closer to her, reaching out to take her in his arms, "Kenzie, I—" Punky bared his teeth, growling. Jake backed off.

"Hey, he doesn't like you," Kenzie noted with a snicker.

"He's just misguided," Jake countered.

"Punky is a trained guard dog. He's reacting to a perceived threat."

The thought of tiny Punky as a trained guard dog seemed so silly that it took everything inside Jake not to bust out laughing.

"I promise you, I'm not a threat." Jake couldn't help the catch in his voice and the grin on his face. Jake had seen a lot of mean animals in his lifetime, but this little guy just wasn't cutting it.

"Punky was raised with German shepherds and he's under the illusion that he's as big and bad as a shepherd. Don't underestimate him. His teeth are sharp and feel like needles digging into your skin. If he sees you as a threat, you might want to, um, retreat."

She stared into Jake's eyes, and he wished that darn dog was back in the SUV. Jake relented and moved away, not because of the dog, but because of Kenzie. He knew she wasn't ready for his sweet words and kisses.

"I'll keep that in mind."

Punky calmed down, licking his chops with a tongue the size of Jake's pinky finger.

"So, if you're going to stay for another day," she began. "You may as well stay for the anniversary. It would be silly for you to leave now when it's so close."

"Makes perfect sense," he added, trying his best to simply agree with everything she said.

"I mean—" She took a breath and let it out, slowly. "What I mean to say is, I need your semen."

HE COULDN'T HELP but chuckle. "Wow, if I'd known all it took was a box of Lucky Charms I would've brought along an entire case."

Her face turned crimson as she held up a hand. "Not *your* semen. I need your stud horse semen…for my mares." She pulled in her chin, and slowed down. "What I'm trying to say is, if your stud offer is still good, I'd like to try it…on my horses."

She shuffled her feet and resettled Punky on her right side.

"I'm sure my stallions would be more than happy to oblige. But why the change of heart?"

"It has nothing to do with my heart, and everything to do with the faulty shipment."

"What happened?" He knew he had to tread lightly here, but he simply had to know the reason.

"The shipment arrived thawed and dead, according to Coco."

Yes!

"Too bad. I hope you can recoup your money. Are you sure you don't want to simply order it again? Maybe from a more reliable source?"

"Haven't had time to think of any of that yet. Besides, I don't want to wait until my mares come into season again. I need them in foal now." She let out a short sharp breath. "I was thinking that maybe we'd start with just Morning Star and my mare, Sweet Girl. We could supervise."

"I'm sure they can handle the deed on their own. Both my stallions understand the difference between working under saddle and the freedom to breed when they're in pasture. Here's my suggestion. Let's give each of my stallions five mares in an enclosed pasture for the next few days. Unless any of your mares are sick, or simply refuse my studs, you'll have the results you're hoping for. I guarantee it."

She thought about his offer for a moment. "But I won't know for sixteen to twenty days after you and your stallions leave whether or not any of my mares will foal."

"It's the same outcome with artificial means. At least this way they're all having a good time. You'll need to put them out today. They need time to get to know each other. Do you have two empty pastures where they can stay out all night?"

She shook her head. "That's where I draw the line. They come in at night, especially since Sweet Girl's accident. No way will I leave her out."

No matter what, she still had to have the last word on the subject. He thought it was simply wasted effort, but at least she'd agreed to the fenced pastures.

"Your call, but I don't recommend it."

She didn't seem to want to give in on this issue. "I know my mares. They're used to their stalls at night."

Jake shrugged, giving in to her demand. "Okay, then let's get started."

"My hired hands and I can work it just fine, thanks. You go on ahead with Joel. Nothing can go wrong for my parents' anniversary. This family has had its fill of wedding, birthday and holiday disasters. This anniversary party has to happen without a hitch."

"I'll see what I can do to help."

"Thanks," Kenzie said, "and thanks for your stallions. When my mares foal next year, please feel free to select whichever one you want. I'll even drive it up to your ranch once it's weaned."

"That's not necessary."

"I insist. It's only fair."

Jake knew she wouldn't take no for an answer. "Then sure. Thanks."

Punky barked a couple times, as if agreeing with everything that had transpired, then Kenzie walked over and hopped back into her sister's SUV. They drove away leaving Jake mystified by the entire turn of events.

"I DON'T GET HER," Jake said as he and Joel worked on erecting a traditional arched, five-foot-wide arbor that Joel had ordered online. It had been a challenge to put any part of it together with keystoned elements and formal style rafter tails, but between the two of them, they were able to figure out what needed to be done and in what order. Once it was standing in the proper place, Zoe, with the help of little Emma, were anxious to add flowers and whatever else Zoe had in mind.

"Who?" Joel asked as he positioned another piece of the puzzle. They'd been at it for almost three hours and they'd hardly seemed to make a dent in the construction.

"Kenzie."

Joel nodded as he drilled in a quarter-inch flathead stainless-steel wood screw. Both men sat or knelt on the ground as they worked. "If she's anything like Callie, it'll take you a while. I found it's best not to underestimate the Grant women or they'll surprise you every time."

"No truer words," Jake said, grabbing a smaller drill bit off the blue tarp that held all their supplies. "She's been nothing but a thorny cactus ever since we were kids. Nothing's changed. And that winning tie we had at the Cowboy Days only made things worse. Maybe if she'd won…and this morning, well, she seemed different. Almost happy that I wasn't leaving."

Joel had carefully laid out all the pieces for the arbor in an organized manner, including every imaginable tool they might need in order to assemble the massive decoration. How Joel thought he could undertake this project by himself was a wonder to Jake. Even with both men working on it for at least four or five hours every day, it was going to be nothing short of a miracle if they got it done in time for the wedding.

The two men worked in a lush grassy area next to the barn. Jake noticed that the barn had been recently painted a deep red, and the ranch house sported not only a beautiful gray-colored tiled roof, but also the house looked as though it had been recently painted as well. He didn't know much about Joel, but from what he could tell, Joel took a lot of pride in his ranch.

Joel stopped working and gazed over at Jake, smirking. "You're falling for her."

Jake didn't particularly want to acknowledge how he felt about Kenzie, not yet anyway.

"She's as ornery as a bull and I'm just now getting over a hurtful divorce. I don't need to jump right back in the frying pan this quickly, but yes, I'm falling for that sweet cactus, hard."

Joel sat back on his haunches. "Is the feeling mutual? Or don't you know?"

Jake pounded in a nail, then stopped working to try to answer Joel's question. He wasn't exactly comfortable with this conversation, but he also knew that was one of the biggest issues of his marriage: his inability to talk about his emotions. Sure he had feelings for Kenzie, big time feelings, but he wasn't ready to take it to the next level, whatever that might be, at least not until they got to know each other better. And under the current circumstances, getting some alone time with Ms. Kenzie Grant, might be as elusive as a white bull.

"I think she has feelings for me, but I can't be sure about anything with her. One minute she wants nothing to do with me, my way of ranching or my stallions. And just when there's no chance, not only does she ask me to stay until Saturday for the anniversary, but she's now willing to couple my horses with hers." Jake put the cordless drill down and readjusted his hat. "Here's the thing—I have a ranch to run in Montana. My brothers are depending on me, especially Lucas. Besides, my dad already has one son off in Portland rebelling against ranching, so he sure doesn't need another son contemplating a move to Idaho."

"Who's to say Kenzie wouldn't consider Montana?"

For all that Joel seemed to know about the Grant family, he sure didn't know Kenzie. Jake was 100 percent certain that Kenzie would never leave her family ranch. That land, that ranch was in her blood, just as certain as his family ranch was in his. They were dedicated, Joel didn't understand that yet. Jake's parents had told him that Joel was relatively new to ranch life. He needed a few more years to understand the deep attachment.

"I appreciate the thought, but I could no more move Kenzie off her family ranch than I could move those mountains." He nodded toward the Teton Range that surrounded the valley. "Any man who got involved with her would have to honor that."

It was the first time Jake fully realized what he was up against. It wasn't natural ranching that Kenzie had been fighting, it was him and all that she stood to lose if she'd let that kiss and her feelings go any further.

Everything suddenly became crystal clear. Their attraction to each other had to stop. It was no good. It would only lead to broken hearts.

"You're probably right on both counts," Joel said, "but from my experience, love has a funny way of making everything work out."

"Wait a minute. Hold your horses, partner. I didn't say anything about love, and especially not for Kenzie Grant. Even if it came to that, which it can't, the two of us could never work something out."

"Then tell me, why didn't you leave early this morning?"

Jake wasn't sure how to answer that. He'd dragged his feet, yes, but he'd never really analyzed why. "I had things to do."

"Like what?"

"Like this arbor. I knew you needed help. You told me so last night."

"Are you sure? 'Cause I don't remember mentioning anything about it."

"You're right. It was Carson. He mentioned something about you needing help with a project. Maybe that's why I wasn't in any big hurry this morning."

Joel reached for another long screw. "You know, you might be right. I may have mentioned it to Carson then. There was a lot happening, seemed the whole town was at Belly Up at one point or another."

"See, I knew it. No way I would have hung around if I wasn't giving you a hand. And there's no one I'd rather help out than the Grants," Jake said, confident now that this was the reason he hadn't packed up and drove on out when he'd had the chance. It had nothing to do with his growing feelings for Kenzie…at least that was what he chose to believe.

"How'd they all do out there today?" Jake asked Kenzie as she closed the gate on the last stall. All the horses had settled in for the night. Sounds of content animals echoed off the walls, with the occasional nicker and hooves scrapping against their bedding. It had been a long day, and Kenzie was really feeling it. She couldn't wait to wash up, change and sit down for a relaxing dinner.

"Contrary to what you may think, my mares don't seem to like your stallions. Try as they may to herd them, the mares were having none of it. Not much wooing going on out there. More like booing if you ask me."

"Don't tell me you watched for the entire time?"

She turned off the lights and they strolled out together, leaving the large doors open. Kenzie noticed the bandage wrapped around Jake's thumb.

"Not the entire time. I had other work to do, but for the hour or so I was there, all my mares did was try to escape your studs. It would've been funny if I wasn't so desperate for them to foal."

"The watched kettle," Jake said, walking right next to her, heading for the main house.

"What about it?"

"You know…the watched kettle never boils."

The sun hung low in the sky, ready to drop behind the mountains. Everything had a golden glow to it, including Jake's face. The man could look so gorgeous at times that he caused her insides to quiver.

She sighed. "I sure hope you're right. Did you have dinner? My mom roasted a couple chickens, and made a fresh blueberry pie. No one makes a better blueberry pie than my mom. Although, I have no idea if those blueberries are organic or not."

"And we were getting along so well."

She stopped, slipped her hands in the back pockets of her jeans and turned to him. "You're right. Sorry. It's been a long day."

"I can tell," he told her, as he gently brushed a smudge off her cheek. "You seem to be wearing it."

She took his hand in hers. "And it seems you are, as well. What happened?"

As soon as he touched her and she him, a rush of warmth dusted her insides, causing her to take a step in closer to him. It was some kind of chain reaction she had no control over. His hand covered hers, sending a shiver down through her. She wanted to fall into his arms and never leave.

"I…um…I hit it with a hammer."

"Ouch," she said, then gently pulled his hand toward her, wanting to kiss it to make the hurt go away.

But he stopped her, quickly slipping his hand from hers.

"Maybe I should pass on that dinner," he said, changing the subject and standing directly in front of her, his eyes searing into hers.

She wanted to look away, but couldn't.

"Don't be silly," she said. "You have to eat."

"I still have Lucky Charms back at the guest-house." His voice was low and sexy. I've been thinking about that box of cereal all day."

"With desire or guilt?"

"One hundred percent guilty desire."

"You know it's not good for you, and in the long run, it can never work out."

"Sometimes you have to take a risk."

"But is it worth it?"

"Oh, yeah," he said, but before Kenzie could say another word, his lips covered hers with such an intensity that it threw her off balance, and she stumbled backward.

The next thing she knew, he had swooped her up in his arms and was carrying her to the guesthouse.

Chapter Nine

The guesthouse was a short distance from the horse barn, just on the other side of a bank of thick trees. All told, about a couple hundred feet. Kenzie felt like air in Jake's arms as she hugged his neck and rested her head on his shoulder. He couldn't believe this was happening, so he didn't want to take any chances by saying something that might pull them both back into reality.

Instead, as he stepped through the trees, intoxicated by the scent of Kenzie's hair, by the feel of her body nestled up against his chest, by the sensual thoughts that had caused his own body to react, reality had already arrived on his front porch.

"Isn't that your mom and dad?" Kenzie asked with a whisper.

Jake stopped dead in his tracks as he watched his dad open the front door to the guesthouse, and his mom sat down on the porch swing. "They haven't seen us yet. We could backtrack to the barn before they—"

"Yoo-hoo! There you are," his mom, Angie, yelled

as she waved her hello. Jake's mom wore her gray hair short, her bifocals had silver wire rims, her clothes were practical and loose-fitting, her boots were always clean and her smile was always welcoming.

Except for maybe tonight.

Jake felt Kenzie's entire body stiffen as she quickly slid from his arms.

"Everything okay?" Jake's dad, Will, shouted as he stepped back out on the porch and started to head down the stairs right for them.

"We're fine," Jake yelled back.

"We'll be right over," Kenzie said in her loudest voice.

"All right, then." Jake's dad, a tall man with salt-and-pepper hair, a stocky build and a dimple in his chin just like Jake's, headed back up the steps, tilted a black suitcase and rolled it inside the open door-way, and within seconds several lights went on both inside and outside of the house.

"I can't believe their timing," Jake whispered to Kenzie.

"It's probably for the best," she murmured back, just as her own dad made his way to the front porch of the guesthouse with the Labs, now rushing to greet Kenzie and Jake.

He didn't want to believe that she could let her emotions go so easily.

She stepped ahead of him, and he gently grabbed her hand, pulling her back. "You can't mean that."

"I don't know what I mean, Jake, but we should let it go."

He didn't want to let it go. Not when they'd come so close to sharing something that might have changed both their lives.

The dogs bumped against Kenzie and Jake eager to get some loving, which they shared without hesitation. Once Dora and Dolly had their fill they took off to greet Will and Angie, as did Kenzie and Jake.

"Are you okay, sweetheart?" Angie asked Kenzie once they hugged and greeted each other. "I saw Jake carrying you. Did you twist your foot or something?"

"Yes," Jake answered when Kenzie hesitated. Then he gave his parents each a warm hug. "She twisted her ankle."

"You let Jake carry you?" her dad asked. "That's a first. Nothing gets this girl down, not even when she cracked a shinbone. Hobbled all the way back to the house from the barn. Then there was the time she pulled out her shoulder and—"

"Dad, I'm fine now," Kenzie said, as she stretched her right foot around to prove to everyone she was fighting fit. "Jake was just trying to help."

His mom looked puzzled, but smiled anyway. She always seemed to take everything at face value, and with three sons, it was probably a blessing. His dad, on the other hand, had always been, and still was a skeptic.

"Don't go puttin' on a happy face for us, young lady." His dad stepped forward. "You set yourself right down on that there swing, prop your foot up, slip out of that boot and I'll get you some ice."

His dad guided her to the swing, and she sat sideways, the pillows between her back and the arm of the swing as she propped up her left foot, carefully slipping off her dusty tan-colored boot.

"I'm fine. Really. Jake just overreacted."

"But wasn't it your right foot that you twisted?" Will asked looking down at Kenzie, grinning.

"Well that just goes to show you how better everything feels." She sat up and pulled her boot back on.

Jake just stood back and chuckled at the whole scene, while his dad gazed over at him with narrowed eyes. Jake could hear the wheels turning and clicking into place. There was no fooling his dad on any level.

"Ya know what, Mildred is getting ready to put dinner on the table," Henry said. "What say we all head on over to the main house before it gets cold."

"That's a good idea," Kenzie said, obviously glad for the distraction.

Once they started for the house, Jake walked next to his mom while his dad, Henry and Kenzie strode on ahead.

"Aren't you guys a couple days early?" Jake asked.

"We sure are," she said. "And from the way you were holding on to Kenzie, we shouldn't have been in such a hurry to get here."

Apparently, his mom was a lot more in tune than he'd ever given her credit for.

BETWEEN TUESDAY EVENING, when Jake's parents had arrived, and late Saturday afternoon, right before everyone left for Saint Paul's, Kenzie had seen Jake exactly three times, and each of those three times she'd been sitting across from him at the dinner table with everyone else who happened to show up. They hadn't had one minute alone since his parents arrived. Between his helping Joel out, all of the ranch work, moving the mares and stallions back and forth…stressing over whether or not they'd coupled…and running her mom back and forth into town whenever Zoe needed her for a last minute decision, Kenzie hadn't had any downtime.

And neither had Jake. His parents were a few years older than Kenzie's and couldn't seem to go anywhere without Jake taking them. Then there was his brother Lucas, who was trying to run their ranch back in Montana on his own, and needed Jake's counsel at every turn.

So when Kenzie and her sisters walked into their parents' room to see their mom in a beautiful white gown, standing in front of a full-length mirror looking even more beautiful than Kenzie thought possible, her emotions came pouring out like rain.

"Oh, Mama, you look gorgeous!" Kayla said, her deep blue eyes misting. She wore her wavy long hair pinned up with tiny pink flowers, the exact color as her silky floral dress that enhanced all her curves.

"Just like a fairy princess," little Emma said, beaming. Her long curly blond hair cascaded down her back, held in place with a white hairband that sported a white silk flower. She looked like a princess in a dress made of yards of sky blue tulle, and dotted with sparkle. Kenzie knew how much Callie loved being Emma's stepmom, and from the way

Emma acted around her, Kenzie knew the feeling was mutual.

"You're lovely, Mom. Just perfect," Callie said, eyes glistening with tears, long chestnut hair flowing around her face and shoulders. She wore a lavender blush, loose-fitting sleeveless dress that accentuated her baby bump. She also wore what looked like brand-new cowgirl boots.

Kenzie knew how much Callie loved being pregnant, and how much she was anticipating this child. Even Emma was excited over the baby brother that was on the way.

"It's not too much? I couldn't decide on white or cream. I ordered it from All About the Bride in town, and Greta, Zoe and Gloria all thought I should go with white."

Greta and Gloria owned the shop. Greta worked out front while Gloria did all the fittings and sewing. Her mom couldn't look any better if she'd been posing for a magazine. The lacy dress draped on her body perfectly. Gloria had once again worked her magic.

"It's ideal for your skin color, Mom. You look positively beautiful. You'll take Dad's breath away," Coco told her, looking amazing in a gray dress that hit just above her knees. She'd even worn heels, which for Coco was a rarity.

"Oh, Mom," Kenzie finally said, while giving her mom a warm hug. "You take *my* breath away."

Kenzie had put off thinking about this day for as long as she could. Secretly, she thought the whole thing was a waste of time and money. Not that she didn't think her parents deserved the wedding reception they'd never had, but in the scheme of things, it all had seemed a bit over the top, with the doves, and the harp player from Boise, and her dad hiring last year's winner of the Lariat Laureate in cowboy poetry to do a reading before Father Beau guided them through their marriage vows. But looking at her mom now, with her daughters and her granddaughter surrounding her with their love, and how beautifully happy and radiant her mom looked, Kenzie decided she'd been all wrong.

This was the absolute perfect way to celebrate forty-five years of an incredible love affair. For the first time in Kenzie's life, she wondered if she would ever celebrate even one year of partnered bliss, let alone forty-five. So far, if the relationship she and Jake had was any indication of her future, the only anniversary she would be celebrating, would be her marriage to the Grant ranch.

THE LAST TIME Jake had been inside a church it was for his own wedding to Heather Montgomery. That seemed like an eternity ago. So much had happened since then, and most of it just in the last couple of weeks.

Jake stood at the back, not sure if he could commit to the entire ceremony by taking an actual seat, even though the ceremony was set to begin in less than ten minutes.

Saint Paul's Catholic Church buzzed with the hushed voices of what had to be the entire populace of Briggs, Idaho. Each pew was filled to capacity, and every man, woman and child seemed eager for the loving couple to appear. A rainbow of pastel-colored flowers adorned the center aisle, the main altar and the two side altars. Twinkling white lights sparkled throughout the church while the scent of incense lingered in the air.

Father Beau, dressed in his best priestly robes, followed by four altar boys carrying large candles, walked out of the side of the sanctuary, stopped, then turned to face the open front doors of the majestic church.

Nothing even came close to this impressive limestone building in Jake's small town, causing him to think the residents of Briggs had been and apparently still were, based on the large crowd inside the church, a deeply religious, strong and tightly knit community of rugged, like-minded individuals. Kenzie and the Grant family fit right in, and from the looks of guests that populated the church, the townsfolk agreed.

"Jake," Kenzie said, appearing from nowhere. "Come sit up front with me."

Then she took his hand, but Jake pulled back.

"I can't," he told her. "I'm not sure I can sit through all of it. Besides, this is a day for your family."

"But you're part of our family. Always have been. My dad and your dad are like brothers."

She pulled on his hand again, and once again he resisted. "Kenzie, I'm not coming with you. I can't sit up front."

She looked positively stunning. He'd only seen her

in a dress one other time and that night they'd shared a moment that had tormented him ever since. If they weren't going to take that moment to the next level, he would just as soon not be around her.

Besides, being trapped inside a church to celebrate a forty-five-year wedding anniversary, while sitting next to a woman he had strong feelings for, so soon after his own failed marriage, only reminded him of how little he knew about relationships.

"Then I'll sit in the back with you."

"You can't do that. You need to be with your family. It's important."

"You're important," she told him while staring into his eyes, and suddenly all his fears and apprehensions disappeared and he gently kissed her hand, feeling her smooth skin against his lips.

He was just about to follow her up to the front of the church when organ music began, and everyone turned their attention to the front doorway. At once Henry and Mildred appeared in the hazy light. They seemed to beam with joy as Henry whispered something to Mildred causing her to smile and say something back that caused him to laugh.

Henry wore a black tuxedo, white shirt, a string tie and polished black boots, while Mildred looked more glamorous then he'd ever seen before. Little Emma stood directly in front of them, dropping rose petals from a white basket, as soon as she began moving up the center aisle, smiling at everyone she passed. Mildred and Henry soon followed close behind.

Jake marveled at their love for each other, the same

kind his parents had. He'd always assumed he'd find that kind of love in his own life. That it would automatically happen without really doing much to find it, but now he realized deep, committed love was more elusive than the wind.

As soon as the happy couple was far enough up the aisle, Kenzie once again asked Jake to follow her to the front, and this time he agreed. As they tried to make their way to their seats, Kenzie stopped and slipped her phone out of the small purse she'd had tucked under her arm.

When she read the text message, her hand went up to cover her mouth, as if she was holding back a scream that wanted to escape.

"What's wrong?" Jake immediately asked, as several men and women began hustling from their seats and rushing out of the doorway that Henry and Mildred had just entered.

"We have to go," Kenzie said, grabbing his hand, then running for the front door. "Our horse barn is on fire!"

KENZIE COULD SEE the black smoke staining the evening sky from two miles out from the ranch. Jake was behind the wheel of her pickup. She'd asked him to drive; what was happening was so personal to her, she couldn't concentrate on anything else. Her brother, Carson, followed somewhere behind them, along with Coco and their parents. Zoe had stayed at the church, along with Father Beau to try and keep everyone calm.

"Tell me that Chad didn't bring the horses in for the night," Jake asked as he kept his hands firmly on the wheel and his eyes straight ahead. He was tearing down the two-way road going over eighty.

Kenzie could barely speak. Her throat felt tight and her chest ached. "I…I brought them in around noon."

Jake slammed the steering wheel with his fist, then sucked in a deep breath and slowly let it out. She'd never seen him so angry.

Then within seconds he began to calm down, and reached for her hand. She gladly took it. "No matter what happens," he began, glancing over at her, "we're going to get through this together."

Kenzie nodded, the lump in her throat the size of a baseball.

"Together," she repeated, as her eyes welled up and he gently squeezed her hand before letting go. He grabbed the steering wheel with both hands, passed a slow driver who'd pulled over, and increased his speed to almost ninety.

Kenzie's nerves were raw as she desperately tried to keep in contact with Chad who had first discovered the fire and called in the fire company. Normally, the local volunteer firefighters could have gotten to the ranch within five or ten minutes, but tonight, every volunteer was at Saint Paul's Catholic Church attending her parents' ceremony.

There were so few fires in Briggs that no one actually stayed at the fire station. The only exceptions to the rule were parade days, rodeos and the annual fair. Since none of those events were taking place today, the station was locked up tight with the trucks, hoses and other equipment inside.

As they were about to turn into the long driveway to the Grant ranch, the local fire truck, with sirens blaring and red lights flashing drove up behind them.

"Thank God," Kenzie said, as Jake eased over to let them by.

Kenzie could see lights from what she assumed was another truck already on the property. The recognition alleviated some of the intense anxiety she felt thinking that no one but young Chad was dealing with the enormity of the blaze.

Jake eased the pickup off the road and drove under the metal arched sign for the Grant Ranch. He followed the speeding fire truck that threw dirt and stones up on Kenzie's truck. Two stones made contact with the windshield, causing tiny fissures that she knew would soon run the length of the window.

Not that it mattered.

Nothing mattered but the lives of the animals.

When they approached the barn, Kenzie's insides shook with fear. The barn was now almost completely engulfed in flames. Fire spilled out from under the roof of the back doorway, the colors of the flames a deep orange at the base, to a bright orange at the tips that licked through the roof.

Night had fallen on the Teton Valley, but the fire illuminated the sky and the surrounding area like nothing Kenzie had ever seen before or wanted to see again. Several firefighters, dressed from head to toe in the appropriate gear, now tugged on a thick fire

hose attached to the truck. Water was finally beginning to spill onto the roof of the barn making a siz-
zling sound that gave Kenzie a deep chill.

Sheriff Jet Wilson and his deputy, Hunter Sears,
walked out in front of Kenzie's slow-moving truck.
The sheriff held up his hands, ordering them to stop,
which Jake obeyed immediately. The deputy came
past them to direct a city ambulance that had also
driven onto the property.

Kenzie slipped off her heels and pulled on the dark
green rubber mud boots she always kept behind the
seats. Jake shrugged out of his suit coat, loosened
his tie and both he and Kenzie exited the truck at the
same time. The roar of the blaze and the sheer vol-
ume of voices yelling orders and warnings hit Kenzie in the gut as panic wracked her body. Still, she
steeled her emotions and lasered in on her purpose:
to sprint for the barn before anyone could stop her,
including Jake. All she could think of was the safety
of her mares and Jake's two stallions.

Headlights distracted her resolve for a moment and
she quickly looked back at the long line of cars and
trucks heading up the drive, stretching up all along
the road. She assumed they were guests from the
church who'd followed them, with Coco's red SUV
leading the way. A light went on inside the SUV and
Kenzie spotted her parents sitting in the backseat,
behind Carson. Coco sat behind the wheel trying to
interpret Sheriff Wilson's hand signals telling her to
stay back.

Sheriff Wilson and Deputy Sheriff Sears did their

best to make sure everyone stopped far enough away from the fire. Kenzie was grateful for that. She didn't want anyone to get hurt, or to interfere with the fire crew.

Unfortunately, her dad wasn't part of the group of folks that were stopped. He'd stepped out of the SUV, then snuck past the Sheriff's watchful eye and was now fast approaching the barn. Carson and Coco had stayed with their mom in the SUV, but apparently their dad had his own ideas.

Kenzie yelled for her dad to come back, but she knew any attempt short of physically restraining him would have no impact. She took off after him, with Jake close on her heels.

"Kenzie, you should go back," Jake told her as he caught up, grabbing on to her upper arms as he pleaded. "It's too dangerous. Please go back."

But Kenzie refused to listen. "And it's not dangerous for you? Those are my mares in that barn, and your stallions. I intend to do everything in my power to make sure they get out." She returned his concern with her own. "You said we were going to get through this together. Did you mean that or were they just empty words?"

Jake looked deep into her eyes, and it was the first time she truly saw the real Jake Scott, the man he'd successfully kept hidden under all his brash bravado—a determined cowboy who would stop at nothing to save what he loved.

"I meant it, Kenzie," he told her still holding on to her arms, then slamming his lips against hers. He pulled away in less than a heartbeat and said, "We're in this together."

Then he took her hand in his, and they ran toward the burning barn, with her dad leading the way.

THE HORRIFYING SCREAMS from the trapped horses sent a shock wave through Jake that pierced his soul. He couldn't listen to it, couldn't bear it, and then was turned away from being able to go near the barn by a determined fireman.

In the midst of all the chaos, and the heart-wrenching screams, he saw Henry break away from another fireman and run toward the barn. Without thinking, Jake went all out after Henry. He could hear Kenzie's voice over the roar of the fire pleading with her dad to come back. Pounding footsteps tried to keep up with Jake, but Jake was no match for whoever was trying to reach him. Pure adrenalin propelled him forward as his own feet barely touched the ground.

Henry couldn't beat Jake's speed and resolve. Before Henry could step one foot into the barn Jake tackled him, pulling him down then shielding him from getting hurt with the fall. Burning cinders struck Jake's back and arm, as he pushed Henry to safety, then he quickly rolled in the dirt to put out the burning embers on his body. When he finally stood, he took a peek into the smoldering barn and saw that all the gates were open, except for one, Sweet Girl's. His stallion, Morning Star stood in front of the gate, as Sweet Girl screamed and kicked at the gate as she rose up on her hind legs.

Jake ran inside, shooed his horse out of the barn and unlatched the gate. Sweet Girl immediately ran out, with Morning Star running along with her. Jake's throat burned from the acrid smoke. Taking a breath seemed impossible. He covered his face with his arms as the flames jumped all around him, licking at his clothes. He ducked out of their way and ran from the barn just as the roof creaked, then collapsed, the force pushing him violently forward as the ground came rushing up to meet him.

Chapter Ten

The last fire truck drove away around midnight, leaving Jake, Coco and Kenzie to deal with the immediate aftermath. Henry had gone off to the hospital in an ambulance, even though he'd protested to everyone around him. The man couldn't understand all the fuss. The prognosis was good, minor burns and a sprained wrist, but his doctor wanted to keep him overnight for observation. Mildred decided to spend the night at the hospital, along with Carson and Kayla.

Jake had several burns on his back, arms and fingers, but fortunately, nothing he couldn't handle. All the burns had been treated and now his main concern was the horses.

Coco had spent the majority of her time treating the mares and stallions for minor burns and scrapes. All the horses had come through the fire a little bit worse for wear, but would be fine. Not the same prognosis for Morning Star. Even Sweet Girl only had a few burns on her back and a badly singed tail.

Morning Star, however, was having a rough time. He'd sustained some major burns on his back and his front legs. His mouth was hurting, as well. Plus, he was suffering from smoke inhalation. Jake couldn't bring himself to leave his side despite Coco telling him many times there was nothing anyone could do but wait.

Apparently, according to Chad, as soon as the fire began, Morning Star had opened about half of the gates. Chad had opened the rest, except for Sweet Girl's gate. The spring on that latch had been changed, and neither Chad nor Morning Star could open it.

"I tried my best, Mr. Scott, but when the barn got too hot and I started choking on the smoke, I had to run out," Chad had told him right before his dad took him home. "I thought I'd locked Morning Star in the corral with the other horses, but he must have opened that latch, as well. I had no idea he'd gone back in until I saw him run out right before you did the same."

Then Chad apologized one more time before he drove away, visibly upset by the entire turn of events.

Jake had tried to tell Chad that he'd been a hero, but Chad wouldn't hear it. Not with Morning Star in such bad shape.

"You should get some rest, Jake," Coco warned him as she clipped some of the hair around Morning Star's burns. She'd already made sure he was hydrated and had given him a shot of penicillin. The mares and his other stallion, Bingo, were huddled together in a tight group in the next corral. None of them had moved since they were rounded up right after the fire had finally been put out.

"I don't want to leave him like this," Jake told her, his heart breaking just watching his horse struggle to keep standing, his breathing audibly labored.

"I gave him a strong sedative to calm him for a few hours. Hopefully, he'll sleep which is what you and Kenzie both need. You must be exhausted."

"I can't—"

"Yes you can, and so can I. I'll sleep in my old room tonight, and check on him periodically through-out the night. It's the least I can do after you stopped my dad from racing into that inferno. Now, I'm going to make sure I soaked his feed enough so it's nice and soft, and that he has access to plenty of fresh water, then I'm heading to bed for a couple of hours. You should, too."

Jake agreed, but he refused to get any sleep until he checked on Kenzie. She'd gone in about a half hour ago, but he knew sleep had been the furthest thing from her mind.

He rapped on her bedroom door.

"Jake. I was just coming out to check on the horses. I can't sleep. I can't do anything but pace my room. I took a shower hoping that would help, but nothing's helped. I have no idea how it could've started. If it hadn't been for Chad's quick thinking, things could have been much worse. How's Morning Star? I should go out and check on him. I—"

He took her in his arms, held her as tightly as he could, wincing at the pressure of his shirt on his burns, and stroked her hair. "Shh," he murmured in her ear. "It's okay. Everybody's okay. We all came through it, and Morning Star is going to be fine. Coco's with him now. There's no need for you to go anywhere but back into bed to get some sleep."

"I can't, not alone. Stay with me tonight."

He pulled away from her and stared at her hard. "Kenzie, are you sure?"

She nodded as tears cascaded down her cheeks. He knew this wasn't how either one of them wanted the night to go, but he also knew if her longing was anything like his, they couldn't be apart. Not tonight. Maybe not ever.

"I need to wash up first," he said. "Most of me is covered in soot from the fire."

"You smell like the burnt barn," she said, apparently trying for a bit of levity.

"You get yourself back in bed, and I'll join you in five minutes."

"Okay," she told him, then she turned and staggered into bed. Dropping on her back, she immediately closed her eyes. Jake knelt down on the floor next to her for a moment and stroked her silky hair off her face. Within seconds she was fast asleep.

Kenzie woke up well before dawn, cuddled up against Jake Scott. The fire and the torturous screams from Sweet Girl still raged inside her head and she sat up with a start, hoping to make the horror stop.

When she opened her eyes, a white full moon glared back at her. She knew she was in her own bed, but it wasn't just a dream.

It had been real.

It had happened.

Her chest still felt tight, making it difficult to breathe properly, to get enough air…the air that reeked of smoke and burning wood. She patted her chest, rubbing it, trying to make the pain go away.

Her limbs began to tingle until Jake's voice cut through her panic. "It's okay, babe," Jake said. "I'm here now. Just take it slow. Breathe through your nose. In and out. In and out. It's over. We're all okay."

She could see his emerald eyes glistening in the moonlight, could see the sweet smile on his face, the dimple in his chin.

She closed her mouth and took one breath at a time through her nose. The tingling began to dissipate as the tension in her body eased up. He continued to guide her through a few more breaths never taking his eyes from hers until she felt she could do it on her own and slumped back down on the bed. Jake lay down next to her and she instantly melted into him, resting her head on his shoulder, her hand on his naked chest.

Still, she couldn't let go of the night, couldn't help thinking about the horrible fire.

"I should check on Morning Star," she told him, trying to pull away, but he held her tight.

"I was just out there. He's doing fine. He's calm, and right now that's how we all need to be. Calm. It won't do any of us any good to stress over what's already happened."

He stroked her head, then rubbed her shoulder, and she began to relax a little.

"I want to know what started it. No one told me what started it."

"They should have an answer in the morning. One of the firemen promised to call you, remember? There's nothing you can do until then."

"Oh, Jake, it was so awful."

"It was, but no one was seriously hurt, and I guarantee that Morning Star will be fine. I'm sure Coco is an excellent doctor."

"She's the best. She'll do everything she can."

"Then there's nothing to worry about."

"The cost of rebuilding the barn will be more than we can afford."

"Your insurance will cover most of it."

"That's the problem. In order to cut costs, I had to increase the deductible. I don't remember what it is, but I know it's over ten thousand. We don't have that kind of cash available."

"Let's talk about all of this in the morning. Everything will still be there waiting for us. We don't have to do anything tonight but sleep."

She knew he was right, and tried to relax into his comforting embrace. Never had she needed someone to lean on like she did tonight. And she couldn't think of anyone in the entire world that she'd rather depend on right now than Jake. His being there for her meant everything.

"Thank you for staying with me," she said.

"I'm here for as long as you need me."

"I may need you for a very long time," she said pushing herself up to see his face in the moonlight.

He sat up and pushed his hands through her hair holding her face, then he leaned in and kissed her. This time there was no pulling away. No second-guessing anything. No thinking about the future. There was only this moment, this second, and nothing could stop them this time. Passion seared through her body as the kiss intensified.

He pulled back to look at her, to run his hands over her breasts, and down to the center of her. "Is that a promise?" he asked, a slight grin turning up his lips as his fingers traced her nipples through her T-shirt. The sensation...pure bliss.

"Yes," she said, putting her mouth back on his, their tongues igniting a deep longing that she'd felt the first time she saw him step out of his truck.

She moved away from his kiss and pulled her T-shirt over her head, tossing it on the floor. He gently cupped one of her breasts, then gently suckled it until she wanted to yell out with pleasure, but before she could, he started on the other. Her mind and body reacted with such intensity, that she couldn't think of anything other than how her body felt at that exact moment...incredible.

"You're more beautiful than I could have ever imagined," he said, his voice almost a whisper as he moved her down on the bed until her head rested on his pillow. "Your skin is like silk. I can't get enough of you."

He slipped out of the boxers he'd worn, then slid her panties down and added them to the pile on the floor. She opened herself to him, revealing everything she had, not wanting to hold any piece of herself back. She wanted to give him everything she had so no matter what happened, this night would end with something good.

His gaze hovered over every inch of her body for what seemed like hours while his hands soothed and caressed her, slowly making love to her, not only with his touch but with his mouth and his tongue until she couldn't stifle the groans that erupted deep within her.

"Let it all go, Kenzie. I'm here to love you," his voice rumbling so low she could barely hear him.

Then, just before her body wanted to shatter with pleasure, he reached to the floor for his trousers' pocket, pulled out a package and slipped on a condom. He entered her slowly, lovingly taking his time with each thrust, until they were both losing control, soaring, while staring deep into each other's eyes.

This time, she knew she could no more push this man away than she could tell him that she wouldn't follow him wherever he wanted to take her. She belonged to Jake Scott, and nothing could change that.

When Kenzie opened her eyes to bright sunlight, the sumptuous smell of coffee and her digital clock telling her it was nine thirty-seven, she didn't budge. She wanted to stay right there for a little longer, safe and warm in her bed. The ramifications of the fire would dominate her entire existence soon enough, but for now she selfishly wanted to take a moment to reflect on what had happened in her bed last night.

The honesty of her emotions.

The memory of his touch, of his kiss.

She was completely and totally in love with Jake Scott, and knew she'd always been in love with him since they were kids.

And now, despite everything that had happened, and the mountain of work that lay in front of her, all she could think of was Jake. She knew if they could get through this "together" they could get through anything.

She turned over to tell him everything she was feeling, to show him one more time before the day began, but of course, he was already gone. She figured he was probably out checking on Morning Star and the damage to the barn.

Reluctantly, she slid out of bed, ready to do the same.

Fifteen minutes later, after calling the hospital to check on her dad, she learned that he was in the process of being released with no other issues than what had been originally diagnosed, Kenzie headed for the back door, coffee mug filled with Jake's organic brew. She had gotten good at making it herself, something she never thought she would be proud of…but she was.

Dora and Dolly had to stay inside for a few days until the barn stopped smoldering, and she could get it fenced off. They weren't happy about the situation, and looked up at her with those big sad eyes of theirs, pleading for her to take them with her.

She bent over to give them some much-needed affection. "It's not safe for you two. I'll try to get it fixed up as soon as I can. I'm so sorry, babies."

She wanted to cry, but instead, she collected herself and walked out the back door.

If it weren't for the acrid smell that still hung in the air, and the fact that the barn was in charred ruins, it would be just another day on the Grant ranch.

However, it most certainly was not, and Kenzie had a difficult time keeping her emotions in check. Just seeing what little remained of the barn, in the light of day, brought her to tears. It was perhaps the single most disturbing event she'd ever endured. And the worst part of it wasn't over. If Morning Star didn't pull through, she didn't think she could withstand the sorrow. And she was certain Jake couldn't.

She spotted the fire chief, Mike Hammer, talking with Carson as they walked from the far side of the destroyed barn.

Kenzie strode up to meet them.

"Do you know where the fire started?" Kenzie asked as they all came to a stop several feet away from the charred ruins.

"Yes, in your feed room," Fire Chief Mike said with certainty.

Kenzie stared at him, at his premature graying hair that his job had most likely helped along. His almond-shaped eyes seemed to accuse her of storing more hay than needed. His perfect nose could undoubtedly detect smoke from a mile away, and pencil-thin lips on a mouth that had just told her, without any emotion, that bales of hay had nearly killed all her horses, her father and Chad. And the man she had recently admitted she loved…the very man who had prompted her to buy all that untreated, combustible hay.

Her heart sank, knowing this would haunt her for the rest of her life.

She should have never listened to him…to his organic methods. She knew better, knew those "natural cowboy ways" didn't work. They were the reason why the ranch was near bankruptcy in the first place, why she'd had to step in and take it over.

She couldn't believe she'd been so quick to let him change her mind with his smooth talking and his darn organic coffee.

"But I've been so careful storing the hay," she argued. "I've checked and rechecked those bales for heat buildup."

A quizzical look swept over Mike's face. "The hay didn't cause the fire. An electrical short inside an outlet in your feed room caused it. That thing had probably been there since this old barn was built some forty-odd years ago. It was hidden for the most part when the new floor was put in. I think that's why it was overlooked."

Carson handed her a document. "It's all in here. The hay was merely fuel."

"What slowed the fire considerably was that fire-retardant floor and walls you put in last year," the fire chief said. "If it hadn't been for that…well, you could have lost much more than just your barn."

"Does Jake know about this? And where is he, anyway?" Kenzie asked Carson.

"I met him and Carson here earlier," Mike said. "We went over everything. I figured he'd want to know, considering it was his horse that seemed to get the worst of it."

"But where is he now?" Kenzie asked.

"I don't really know," Carson said. "Mike and I went over to the hospital for a while to check on Dad. We got back about a half hour ago and apparently Jake had loaded up both his horses and left."

Carson's words hit Kenzie right in the gut.

"Did he mention to anyone where he was going?"

"No, but I know he had to get back to his ranch for a roundup," Carson said.

"But he wouldn't leave without telling me. I know he wouldn't."

"Well, speaking of leaving, I'd best be heading out. Got a lot to do over at the station today. Let me know if you two need anything else," Fire Chief Mike said. "Really sorry about your barn."

"Thanks," Carson said, as he and Kenzie watched him leave. Kenzie hung back trying to absorb everything she'd just learned.

"How are you holding up?" Carson asked once the fire chief drove away.

"Not very well," Kenzie admitted. "Oh, Carson, it's all my fault. I sensed there was a problem with the electricity—there'd been some flickering and inconsistencies—but I didn't stop and ask Dad to check it out. The fire could've been avoided if I'd just taken the time to tell him. I get so busy and have to be right about everything that I can't see what's in front of me. And now Jake probably hates me. Poor Morning Star—"

"Nobody hates you, Kenzie. We all know how hard you work, how hard it is to run a ranch. Trust me, nobody's blaming you for anything."

"But they will, and they should. I can't do this. I can't be in charge of this ranch. This just proves it."

She'd known there was something wrong with the electricity in the horse barn for several days, but would kick herself forever for not taking the time to get it seen to. She'd lost her priorities.

Tears rolled down Kenzie's cheeks as the sights and sounds from the fire replayed in her head.

"You can't always avoid disaster. It's part of life, and nobody knows that better than I do."

Carson took her in his arms, and she rested her head on his shoulder. As far back as she could remember Carson had always been there for her, and for all of her sisters. He was the big brother that every girl wanted: kind, compassionate, loving and most of all, nonjudgmental. He always seemed to know exactly the right thing to say whenever any of them needed his older-brother wisdom.

And at the moment, Kenzie needed it more than ever.

"Your rodeo accident was different. You couldn't avoid what happened."

Carson had gotten tangled up on a wild horse named Red Comet and couldn't get himself free when the horse bucked him off. Barney, the rodeo clown, ran out to help and Red Comet kicked him so hard,

Barney almost died. Carson had always blamed himself and still did at times. But he also knew that he wasn't on his game that night, wasn't focused because of a bombshell his ex-fiancée had dumped on him right before the ride.

"I almost cost someone his life. That qualifies, believe me. But I learned a big lesson from that. We Grants know how to pick ourselves up and keep going, no matter what. And I expect nothing less from you...especially you. You're my hero, Kenzie Grant. In just a few short years you made this ranch profitable again."

"And last night I tried to burn it all down."

"You don't know that Dad or anyone else would have found that short. According to Mike, that outlet must have been that way since it was put in. It was just a matter of time until it sparked a fire. We were all just lucky you added that fire retardant flooring last year or who knows what might have happened. You saved lives, Kenzie. You're a hero."

"Jake doesn't think I'm a hero, or why else would he have left? I thought we were...well, I'm, well, I'm—"

He gently picked up her chin with his finger to gaze into her eyes.

"Don't tell me you've fallen for that Mother Nature Boy?"

Kenzie nodded. "And now what? What do I do with all these feelings I have for him?"

"If I know anything about guys, I'd bet you my National Buckle that he feels the same way about you."

"Then why did he leave?"

"I can't answer that, but let's give him the benefit of the doubt before you go thinking the worst. Now let's dry those tears and get to work. We've got ourselves a new barn to build."

But Jake had left without even saying goodbye.

He knew that the fire and his wounded stallion were her fault. He'd been with her when the lights flickered a few days ago. He knew she should have said something to her dad, to someone who knew how to wire a barn.

No wonder Jake was gone. If anything happened to Morning Star he would never forgive her, and she didn't know if she could bear that.

Chapter Eleven

Two days and two nights had passed since the fire, all of it pretty much in a blur as Kenzie dealt with the insurance company and then had meticulously gone through the books three times to see if she could find a way to come up with the needed ten thousand dollars to pay the insurance deductible that now loomed over her head.

She'd managed to remember to eat a little, with some prompting from her mom. Sleeping was the most difficult of all. Her dreams were horrific, with memories of the fire creeping in every time she closed her eyes...and while she lay awake in between nightmares, all she could fixate on was the sweet lovemaking with Jake, and then, well, then she couldn't sleep at all.

This morning when she'd used the last of Jake's coffee beans for a final pot of coffee, she'd just about fallen completely apart, unable to stop the sobs and the tears from pouring out.

Her dad had stepped up and wrapped an arm around her and held her until her sobs diminished.

"I'm sorry, Dad, but I don't know if I can do this." Not alone, anyway. Her heart ached for Jake and she had a feeling it always would. She wanted him back in her bed, by her side, loving her again. She'd picked up her phone several times to call him, to plead with him to return to Briggs, but then couldn't call, knowing he had to come to this decision on his own, regardless of what she said. She knew his heart had already been broken once, and he was probably trying to make sure it wouldn't be broken again.

Kenzie understood all of this consciously, but her own heart was breaking and she didn't know if she could stand the pain.

"We'll get through this. I promise." Her dad always liked to look at the rosy side of a mess, even if everything seemed bleak. After all, not only had the barn been destroyed, but her parents' anniversary party, and their renewal vows never took place. A lot of money spent for nothing. Sill, her dad seemed to refuse to let any of it get him down. Her mom was reacting the same way.

"This time, I'm not so sure," Kenzie said, still holding on to her dad a little longer.

Her dad finally backed away and held Kenzie by her arms and gazed into her eyes. "Kenzie Grant, you're stronger than you give yourself credit for, so you believe me when I say that I *know* we'll get through this…you'll get through this. Your mom and I may not say it out loud often enough, but we're mighty proud of you, mighty proud. What you've done with this place has been a downright miracle, and you know that even though I invited Jake here it was never meant to diminish anything you've already accomplished. The barn burning down, well, that can be replaced. The important thing is nobody was hurt, and all the horses, even Jake's horse, are gonna be fine. Your sister guaranteed it. We'll rebuild and don't you worry, the barn will be better than ever. That's a promise."

Kenzie sniffled a few more times, then moved away and reached for a paper towel from the roll on the counter to mop up her tears. The roll sat next to the sink, which was directly in front of double windows. When she glanced out the windows it took a moment to register the long line of ranch trucks, heavy duty trucks and cars that were headed for the burned-out shell that was once the Grant horse barn.

Blinking, she reminded herself it was daylight and she wasn't dreaming. Maybe she was having a nervous breakdown and replaying that scene from the night of the fire in some kind of hallucination. It sure looked like the night of the fire when it seemed as if the entire town had shown up to help with putting out the fire.

"Will you get a load of that?" her dad said. "What is all that?"

"So, you see it, too? I'm not imagining this?"

"I see it, too, but doggone it, I don't believe it!"

Kenzie followed her dad outside, and the first thing Kenzie recognized was Jake's truck and horse trailer at the head of the long line of vehicles.

What?

Her dad held her hand so tightly it almost hurt as she accompanied him to the head of the line and right to Jake's rig just as he stepped out. A big grin on his absolutely, adorably handsome face. Soon Kenzie's mom had joined them.

"What is all this?" her mom asked.

"I got a feeling we've got us some mighty good neighbors, Millie. Better than we ever knew," her dad said with a hitch to his voice. Kenzie knew this outpouring of love was much more than she or her parents could ever have hoped for.

Kenzie's heart swelled at seeing Jake again, especially heading up the long line of vehicles behind him. She wanted to rush right into his arms, but she held back, not knowing how he felt about her...about everything that had happened.

"Surprise!" he shouted, looking confident and happy. His wide grin reflecting everything she was feeling.

"What is all this?" Kenzie asked, hoping that this contingency of townsfolk and tools and wood was the answer to her prayers.

"I didn't want to tell you until I had it all organized, which, believe me, took some doing."

"Jake Scott, what have you done?" her mother asked, as she held up a hand to shade her eyes from the sun while gazing out at the majority of their friends exiting their vehicles, wearing work clothes and carrying tools, coolers, wood beams and everything else to rebuild a barn.

The other cars and trucks had stopped, and she

spotted Joel, and her brother Carson, and Milo Gump, and Fire Chief Mike, and Amanda Gump, and the extended Granger family. From the looks of it, just about everyone they knew had driven onto their property.

Her mom stepped right up and hugged Jake, then her dad. Jake beamed with pride.

"I haven't seen one of these in twenty years, ever since old man Gabaur lost his barn in a lightning storm," Kenzie's dad told Jake.

"It's a good old-fashioned barn raising," her mom said. "Am I right?"

Jake stared at Kenzie over her mom's shoulder, looking proud and humbled at the same time.

Kenzie shook her head, not really believing this was actually happening, either. Jake hadn't left after all. He'd been busy planning this surprise.

He said, "I should have let y'all in on things, but I couldn't until I was certain it would happen. If it hadn't, I thought it might be devastating for you all, and you've been through so much already."

Her parents headed out to greet family and friends. Kenzie stood her ground and crossed her arms over her chest, not knowing if she should cry for joy or be mad as a wet hen that he'd let her think he'd gone back to Montana.

Her mom marched right over to where some of the folks were gathering behind some of the pickup trucks unloading coolers and picnic baskets no doubt filled with food, and helped set things up on tailgates. Dad greeted everyone with a firm handshake and a pat on the back. Kenzie caught him wiping his eyes every now and then, emotions bubbling up faster than he could control them.

Jake now stood in front of Kenzie, still grinning.

Putting her last ounce of strength into her voice, she said, "I thought you'd left me. I thought you went back home."

"I'm sorry. I should have called, should have come over, but I couldn't, not without knowing for certain that I could make this all work. I've been staying at Joel's. He offered his barn for Morning Star and Bingo. I took him up on his generous offer. Coco is a miracle worker. Morning Star is eating again. It's going to take a while, but he's going to be just fine. Joel helped me pull all this together, he and Wade Porter. We were so caught up in calling everyone and getting the word out, and then we had to pick up the supplies, and schedule big equipment—plus the Dumpsters—to clear out all the burned wood. It literally took up every single minute of my time. I don't think we really ever slept. I should have made the time, I know, but I wanted to surprise you and your parents. And I was afraid it would all fall apart, so I decided to wait until I knew for sure that it would happen."

As the words spilled out—more words at one time than she ever remembered coming out of those perfectly kissable lips on the absolutely beautiful cowboy who stood in front of her, like some knight in shining armor. Better still, he was her strong-willed, determined, natural cowboy in work clothes, ready to dig in and make a miracle happen.

Her heart filled with more love than she thought possible.

"Still mad?" he asked, opening his arms to invite her in closer.

"Nope. Proud. Happy. Missed you more than anything."

"Then come on over, 'cause for as much as you missed me, I missed you even more. I realized something while I was away from you for these last two days. Something that I hope will help us get through this and anything life throws our way. I love you, Kenzie Grant. I've loved you ever since I first met you with your doll in your back pocket and your defiant attitude. I love everything about you and I especially love your feisty spirit. I don't know what the future holds for us, or if you feel the same way, but I can't keep my feelings inside one more minute. That barn fire taught me more than it took away. Love is all that matters, and I love you."

She fell into his arms and buried her face in his shoulder, wanting to stay right there forever. She didn't know how they would ever make this work, but she knew for certain, they'd find a way.

"I love you too, Jake Scott, like crazy."

He picked her up and twirled her around letting out a loud *woop*!

Then he carried her off to a nearby tree, out of sight of the crowd buzzing with excitement, with some of the men and women already shouting orders to unload the supplies. In the distance she heard the start of the demolition equipment's engine, the leveling of the burned wood about to be torn down so the new barn could be framed.

He finally placed her on her feet, her back against the trunk of one of the bigger trees on the ranch. "I called my brother Curt and we finally had one of those long brotherly talks. Lucas was part of it, as well. Skype is a beautiful thing. We must have talked for three hours, about everything from my marriage to growing up on the ranch to Curt's meltdown. It really cleared the air."

"I'm so glad. Is Curt still in Portland?"

"Nope, by now he should be back home on our ranch. He admitted that the city was about to choke him to death and he'd been wanting to come home but his pride was getting in the way. He confessed that he just wasn't cut out for anything but ranching. He sounded so happy that I had to believe him. He said he couldn't wait to get started on the roundup."

More joy filled her heart with everything Jake was saying. "Does this mean you can stay awhile?"

He nodded. "Looks like you're stuck with this ol' ornery cowboy for as long as you want me here. I meant what I said when I told you we were in this together, babe. You and me. Together we can do anything. Starting with rebuilding your barn, an even bigger barn this time with all the bells and whistles. And maybe, as long as we're at it, we can start that house you wanted to build up on the hill, with the view of the entire ranch."

Kenzie pulled him to her, wrapping one leg around

his to pull him in even tighter, his hard angles fitting perfectly against her soft curves. "You mean it?"

He nodded, smiling. "I most certainly do. We can do this."

"Together," she said, then she kissed him, while tapping into her inner alley cat.

"Um," he moaned, pulling away for a moment to gaze into her eyes. "I think we're on to something here."

Epilogue

Two Months Later

"You're sure?" Kenzie asked, then squealed when Coco nodded.

"Definitely. Every single one of them. Your mares will foal in the spring just like you planned, even Sweet Girl. Jake's stallions did their jobs well."

The two women hugged for a long time, savoring the moment.

"It's nothing short of a miracle, given all that those animals have been through."

"Mother Nature probably had a little something to do with it…along with those two very fine stallions."

Kenzie gazed out at the two pastures, Bingo in one with five of the mares and Morning Star, who had now almost completely recovered, in the other with Sweet Girl, and the rest of his mares.

Morning Star had made a miraculous recovery thanks to the diligence of Coco's expert hand and Kenzie finally felt like she could take a breath, enjoy what they'd achieved and believe they all had a promising future...horses *and* humans.

Coco glanced at her watch. "We better get a move on or we'll be late."

Both women were dressed casually in their finest ranch wear, as they climbed into Coco's SUV along with Dora and Dolly and headed off to Joel and Callie's. The family was now ready to conclude the ceremony that had been interrupted by the fire.

"I take it Mom and Dad have already left?" Coco asked once they were on the main road.

Kenzie nodded. "Bright and early this morning. Dad said Mom seemed happy their anniversary party isn't such a big deal this time, with only family and a few close friends."

Kenzie was just happy they were doing it at all after the last attempt. And it felt good, part of putting that horrible day behind them. The beautiful new barn was now back up and better than ever, a perfect time for a party.

As they pulled up to the Double S Ranch and parked, Kenzie was surprised at the amount of cars and pickups that were parked at all angles, everywhere there was space.

"Looks like this party is a bit bigger than we thought."

"You know how this town is. They love to celebrate. Most of them probably invited themselves. And look over there." Coco pointed to the side of the ranch house, where at least three cooks stood moving chicken and beef around on large black barbeques, white smoke wafting up all around them. "Aren't they from Sammy's Smokehouse in town?"

"This is crazy. I thought Mom just wanted something simple?"

"Her friends must have had other ideas."

The two women chortled with delight as they parked and then followed everyone over to the arbor where the ceremony would take place, with Father Beau giving them his blessing.

Kenzie searched the area for Jake and smiled when she saw him coming out of the house, looking as striking as ever, wearing what appeared to be new darkwash jeans and a deep green shirt that complimented his gorgeous eyes. Was that a new cowboy hat? And boots? He seemed more dressed up than she'd seen him since he'd arrived in Briggs, and wondered what was up.

But before she could ask him anything, her mom and dad walked to the arbor where Father Beau stood waiting to give them his blessing. Mom looked beautiful in a new pair of jeans, a fringed jacket, a cream-colored straw cowgirl hat and deep red cowgirl boots. Her dad looked charming in his pressed jeans, crisp white shirt and string tie. Their hats actually matched, and if Kenzie remembered right, they'd had matching hats when they'd first gotten married. Her dad had picked them up in town at Hess's Department Store. It was her mom's very first cowboy hat. Apparently, he'd done the same thing this time, no doubt for good luck.

The blessing took all of ten minutes, and afterward

everyone clapped and cheered and got right down to the important stuff...the celebration. A small traditional country band played an old Johnny Cash song while her mom and dad greeted their friends.

Jake stepped up close to Kenzie and handed her a longneck bottle of beer. Kenzie tapped his bottle. "To my mom and dad and another forty-five years!"

They both took a healthy pull on their beers.

"Feeling good?" he finally asked.

"The best," she told him, genuinely meaning it. His brothers had taken over running their family ranch, which allowed Jake to stay right there in Briggs, on the Grant ranch. He'd recently made a quick trip home to make sure everything was going well, which it was, better than expected, and to gather up more of his things. His stallions stayed behind, appeasing any apprehensions Kenzie might have had that he wouldn't return.

"Me, too," he said, then he set his bottle down on one of the long wooden tables set up for dinner. To Kenzie's complete surprise, while everyone was busy cheering on her mom and dad, Jake reached into his back pocket and pulled out a tiny blue velvet box.

A rush of anticipation swept through her. They'd gotten very close in the last couple of months, spending all their free time together during the day, and essentially living together in the guesthouse at night. She'd taken their love affair a day at a time, never knowing when he'd tell her he had to leave, had to return to Montana, permanently.

"Jake, what's going on?"

"Kenzie Grant, hush for once and give me a chance to say what I've been practicing for weeks now."

She bit her lower lip and waited. Then she watched as her cowboy went down on one knee, while opening the little box at the same time.

"My beautiful, loving, amazing Kenzie Grant, the woman who takes my breath away and makes me a better man. Will you make me the happiest guy on earth and marry me? 'Cause I don't want to live another day without my favorite cowgirl by my side... without you as my wife."

He waited as she stared at the gorgeous ruby ring encircled with tiny diamonds, then she looked into his sparkling green eyes, which gleamed more than any gemstone ever could.

Her eyes welled up with tears.

"Well?" he prompted. "You're killin' me here..."

She took a deep breath, trying to relax her throat as tears streamed down her face, then she smiled like she'd never smiled before. Laughing, she said, "Yes, I will be your wife now and forever, despite your stubborn *natural ways*." He stood and she continued. "You're stuck with this here cowgirl...but then I guess you knew that back when we were kids. I never left you alone then, and I certainly won't be leaving you alone now."

He took the ring out of the box and slipped it on her finger, and she let out a sobbing giggle. She was so happy, she could barely keep from leaping into his arms right there, with everyone around them. When they embraced, she melted into a tantalizing kiss, and couldn't help the laughter that erupted deep within her.

Within seconds the air around them erupted with cheers, whistles and applause. At first she thought it was for her mom and dad, but when Kenzie and Jake pulled apart, she realized it was for them. All the guests, along with her siblings, his parents and her parents now surrounded them. Nothing ever got past the residents of Briggs, Idaho, and as sure as the day was long, Kenzie's marriage proposal from Jake Scott would not be one of them.

He leaned back to get a better look at her. His face beaming. "Are you laughing at me, Kenzie Grant? Laughing at my kiss?"

"I sure am, Jake Scott. You're the best time I ever had."

* * * * *

If you enjoyed this romance set in the quaint, rustic town of Briggs, Idaho, check out other titles from USA TODAY *bestselling author Mary Leo:*

FALLING FOR THE COWBOY
AIMING FOR THE COWBOY
CHRISTMAS WITH THE RANCHER
HER FAVORITE COWBOY
A CHRISTMAS WEDDING FOR THE COWBOY